The Boat

Jim Markson

Disclaimer:

This book is a work of fiction. The characters in the book were fabricated from the author's imagination and are not intended in any way to represent real people, living or dead. The places, events, and incidents of the book are either the work of the author's imagination or used fictitiously. Any resemblance to actual persons, business establishments, events or locales, is purely coincidental.

Note:

All statements of fact, opinion, or analysis expressed are those of the author and do not reflect the official positions or views of the CIA or any government agency. Nothing in the contents should be construed as asserting or implying U.S. Government authentication of information or Agency endorsement of the author's views. This material has been reviewed by the CIA to prevent the disclosure of classified information.

Dedicated to my wife,
the only girl I've ever loved.

Acknowledgments

As may come to light if this book sells worth a damn, there were some issues associated with the government's review of my first fictional book, *An Average Spy*. In the most difficult of these times, I was provided invaluable emotional and legal support by several great lawyers, the first being Dan Schwartz and Brenda Gonzalez of the law firm Bryan Cave. Later on, Phoenix Harris of Harris & Carmichael came to my rescue. They are great people, represent the best traditions of our legal system, and it is an honor to be able to publicly thank them. I am not sure I would have been able to persevere without them.

The seed of this book started with my brother, and his love for building and sailing small boats. My sisters provided critical help with editing and creative review. My wife and children patiently endured the many troubles and trials that accompanied my pursuit of professional writing. I could not have been blessed with a better family, and thank you all for your support.

And most importantly, I want to thank the Lord, whose patient love I have spurned repeatedly, yet found always waiting whenever I opened my heart and eyes. I have been a jackass on too many occasions, so let me once do it right and say thank you for all my blessings.

I

"The bag … get the bag!" Mike Kelly yelled to his brother, who was hanging onto the opposite side of the small capsized boat.

John could barely hear his brother's shouts over the wind and cascading waves, and what little he could hear was rendered unintelligible by floating, busted equipment banging against the hull of the boat. Despite the cold chaos and growing darkness, they still had eye contact, and John, extending his left arm out, bent at the elbow with his palm facing up, signaled that he had no idea what his brother was saying.

"The bag … get the fucking bag!" Mike repeated, shouting with all his body and motioning to a bag floating away from the boat and momentarily silhouetted by the moonlight on the top of a three-foot wave two body lengths away from John. Still not hearing Mike, but understanding his general intent, John looked in the direction of his brother's gesture and saw the bag just before it slipped back down the far side of the wave. The upside down bag was white, the same type typically used to line a kitchen garbage can, but it was firmly tied halfway up its length, and the air caught in the top was acting as a sail, carrying its precious cargo hidden below the water farther from the boat with each successive wave.

Finally realizing that his brother wanted him to leave the relative safety of the capsized boat and swim to the rescue of the escaping bag, John turned back to look at his brother with bemused incredulity, simply shaking his head to gesture a firm "no." Despite his brother's exhortations and obviously twisted priorities, John Kelly would not be fetching his brother's bag of goodies. *Maybe,* he thought, *we should focus on righting this boat?*

II
Earlier in the day

It was after sunset, and the two brothers were technically in the Gulf of Mexico, even if it was only half a mile southeast of the mouth of Tampa Bay. They were thirteen hours into the first day of an eight-day adventure race from Tampa to Marathon Key called the EcoLoco Challenge, and things weren't looking good. The boat was a nine-foot nutshell pram, a sailboat that John had been building for years and had finally finished just before going off on his most recent deployment to Afghanistan. It was the type of boat used to teach young kids how to sail in a mild breeze on a sunny afternoon in a lake or protected bay. It was barely big enough to hold both Mike and John, and ridiculously overweight when you added all the supplies and equipment needed for the eight-day race. Mike was amazed he hadn't been asked more questions at the equipment inspection prior to the start of the race.

The weather had been the worst in the twelve-year

history of the event. A front was passing through and appeared to have been timed to coincide precisely with the sunrise starting launch of the race. As the red ball of fire rose out of the east, below the Skyway Bridge that defined the mouth of Tampa Bay, it was quickly hidden behind fast-moving gray and misty clouds looming ominously close to the water. A bagpipe began its eerie wail, announcing the official start, the sound banking off the low ceiling of clouds, and the crews of larger boats began to push their crafts from the beach with confidence and shouts of enthusiasm. Many others, however, the first-timers as well as some of the more experienced, hung back with second thoughts about the wisdom of launching in such conditions. Some waited a few hours, others waited till the next day, and a full fourth, maybe the wisest, decided they could wait until next year.

The cold front was slowly moving south, the same direction as the racers, and there was no way to know if it would hang with the competitors the whole way, resulting in a week's worth of black-and-blue beatings, or move out smartly, leaving behind blue skies and favorable winds. At the beach launch, however, things were dismal. The winds were twenty-four knots and right into the face of the racers, making it particularly difficult to even get off the beach. While four-foot waves are nothing for most boaters, this race was specifically designed for small boats; many of the competitors were in small single kayaks, and a wave half the length of the boat was a formidable source of power. While the outriggers and catamarans seemed to have an easier time, the strong wind on the nose beat several of the single-hulled sailboats right back into the shore before they could ever gain enough distance to begin maneuvering and tacking into the stiff wind.

Mike and John surveyed the scene without conversation. This was their first time at the event and they didn't know any of their fellow competitors, many of whom were obviously experienced veterans. Some of the single sailors and kayakers the brothers assessed as having the most experience were quietly hanging back, looking for the sun behind the gray clouds, and watching the direction of the wind and the waves. For half an hour the two leaned against their small sailboat saying nothing, just watching what the others were doing.

While John had built the boat, the idea of entering the race had been Mike's, and he had undertaken all the preparations with the understanding that his brother was coming along strictly as unprepared support crew. It wasn't the small boat's maiden sail, but it was the first time she had ever been in open water, and would also be the first time that anyone other than John had sailed her.

"Well, Skipper, what do you say? Call it a day and go have a beer?" John asked without much hope. He had suffered more than his fair share of being miserable in the army, and his lust for adventure had been sated over the years, replaced by an appreciation of the comforts of civilized life.

Mike looked at him without saying anything, shook his head quietly, and smiled as he muttered, "Fuck that; let's get this party started." The two easily pushed the small boat off the beach, waded out into the bay until the water was almost up to the waist of their dry suits, and then jumped in simultaneously on opposite sides of the boat. Mike took out the oars and easily bolted them into their locks. With his back against the wind and his face toward the beach, he began rowing as the small boat was tossed up and down by the incoming waves.

The chop of the waves made it hard to get a steady bite of water with the oars, but they were making progress and not being beaten back into the beach like many others. Mike rowed until they had an extra measure of maneuvering room, then stopped and stowed the oars. John admired Mike's ability handling a boat in which he had never spent any time, and as Mike quickly mounted the small mast, he instructed John to switch places as he raised the sail and moved to the back of the boat. On the way, Mike dropped down the centerboard of the boat and, once in the stern, mounted and bolted the tiller in place. He then pulled in the main sheet of the sail as he turned the boat to run parallel to the beach, which constituted the western lip of Tampa Bay.

The brothers made good time with the strong wind, but the heavy chop made everything more difficult. With each wave, a significant amount of water was splashed into the boat, and John took up bailing duty, amazed at the effective bailer Mike had made out of an old milk jug. The bailer was securely fastened to the base of the mast so that it could reach wherever needed, was always within easy access, but was easily stowed if they ever got to a point of smooth sailing.

They spent the next several hours running parallel to the beach, but, even with the centerboard, the wind and the waves would eventually push the boat too close to the beach. They would then have to essentially reverse course, tacking back into the wind to gain some distance away from the rocky beach. It was fairly simple sailing, but the wind and the chop kept both the brothers busy, and there wasn't much said.

After their second tack, probably about 0900 hours, Mike leaned forward and pulled a small insulated cooler bag from under the center plank of the boat. With his foot holding the tiller, he unzipped the bag and pulled out a white garbage bag. John watched with amazement as Mike untied the bag and pulled out a bottle of Wild Turkey bourbon, which he nimbly tucked under his steering leg as he tied the bag back up and put it back into the open cooler, pushing the latter back under the center plank.

"Here's to fair sailing," Mike said, his second sentence since they had left the beach. He unscrewed the cap, hoisted the bottle, and took a swig.

"What are you doing?" John replied with concern and bewilderment.

"You prefer vodka? "Mike asked. "I got some of that too. Even got small bags of weed - haven't had any of that stuff since we were teenagers! But we'll need fairer sailing before we get into any of that." Mike smiled as John looked on, speechless. "Okay, then, Turkey it is!" he said and took a longer pull off the bottle and screwed the cap back on, handing it to his brother.

Based on John's countenance, Mike imagined the questions swirling faster than the winds coming at them off the starboard side. They had spent less and less time together as they had grown older, mostly as a result of John's military career. And undoubtedly John's own mind was twisted in ways he would never fully understand. Yet, here he was, looking at his younger brother, but wondering who the madman steering their small boat was.

"Quite a neat little trick, your refreshments and all," was all John could say.

Mike noted the tone of concern and disapproval. He didn't want to get into a fight with his brother; he wanted to have a good time, maybe one last good time together. "Aw, come on, man, lighten up. When was the last time we were out together sailing? You don't want any, I don't mind. If you get worried about my skippering skills, the tiller is all yours. Besides, it's not like we're gonna have a real party out here with this wind." Mike reached forward, took another quick swig, and said, "Lets get ready to tack and see if this time, on the way back, we can make it all the way up the beach and line up with the harbor mouth." John didn't respond, suddenly preoccupied with deeper concerns about the changes in his brother.

The boys made the tack without incident and spent an hour or so gaining several hundred yards from shore, before turning yet again and running a line parallel to the beach. The wind had changed slightly, and they were running with the main sail a little less tight; making it to Mullet Key at the southwest corner of the bay in a couple of hours didn't look like a problem. John said nothing as Mike occasionally pulled the bottle of Wild Turkey out from under the center plank and had a swallow. The sky was still overcast, and, as the temperature was moderate, they unzipped the front of their dry suits, but a damp chill set in shortly thereafter. John finally relented and took a pull from the bottle offered by his brother. The fire in his mouth warmed his throat and body as it descended to his gizzards.

It was mid-afternoon when they beached the boat on the small spit of land known as Mullet Key. With the boat secured, they walked together to the southeastern tip of the island, surveying the relatively small channel they needed to cross in order to begin the real part of their journey. The crossing they gazed at was known as Egmont Channel, and while it was not particularly wide, navigating it was a challenging task for the small boat. The water depth dropped from an average of twenty feet they had been sailing in thus far, to over sixty feet, and it ran fast, as all the tide water of Tampa Bay moved in and out twice a day. In addition to the swift currents, the chop changed to bigger, rolling waves that gained steam as they barreled their way down the channel, which made navigation a greater concern, as no land markings would be visible when the little boat was in the trough of these rollers. These concerns were amplified by the fact that the channel was used by huge cargo ships entering and leaving

Port of Tampa and, while a sailboat generally had the right of way, if they found themselves in the path of one of these behemoths, there simply was not enough room for the bigger ships to alter course; the small boat would be doomed.

With the boat beached, the far side of the channel was approximately a mile away from where they stood and was marked by small, deserted Egmont Key. Several hundred yards long, Egmont essentially divided the mouth of Tampa Bay in half, with the water on the other side of the island constituting the Southwest Channel, twice the width of the Egmont Channel, but much shallower in depth and typically used by yachts and pleasure craft.

Mike assessed the crossing of the first channel as probably the most dangerous part of their journey. The crossing was complicated greatly by the fact that they would essentially be sailing directly into the wind, and if they were forced to tack, a term used when a boat zigzagged into the wind, they risked the potential of luffing, with sails flapping uselessly as the bow of the boat pointed directly into the wind. Such an event posed a moment of complete vulnerability... to the fast tides and big rollers that would be hitting them broadside, and the even bigger cargo ships that had no brakes even if they saw the little nine-foot boat trying to cross the channel.

One thing in their favor was an abundance of daylight; it was still mid-afternoon and Mike hoped to reach Egmont and cross above the north side of the key before it was close to dark. Once through the first channel, they would then complete the less adventurous two miles across the Southwest Channel over to Anna Maria Island, which essentially constituted the mainland of the Florida Peninsula. On the other hand, they had missed slack tide by over an hour, and while the tides were not yet at full speed, they were gaining momentum with every passing minute.

The brothers walked back to the boat and then dragged it through the shallow waters to the very tip of Mullet Key. Mike had brought much less safety equipment than required by the race organizers, but one of the items he did bring was a set of binoculars. He couldn't help but look across the bay and gaze on the majority of competitors who had taken the option of crossing the breadth of the bay at the start of the race, rather than paralleling the contour of her mouth as he had chosen. This was likely to cost the others more time as they tacked back and forth into the wind across the entire bay, but they were now enjoying the comfort of maneuvering room and avoiding the vortex of tides, waves, and big boats at the harbor's mouth.

Mike brought the focus of the binoculars back to the route across Egmont Channel, and seeing no large ships in either direction, put the binoculars back into the case and tossed them into the buoyant equipment bag in the front of the boat. "Yippie-ki-yay, big brother, it's time to tighten up your chinstrap and see what we're made of."

Five minutes after pushing off and aiming northeast for the top side of Egmont Key, the brothers started to feel the strong outgoing tide pulling them south, toward the Gulf of Mexico. The big rolling waves were actually a pleasant change from the banging chop they had experienced prior to this point, but as they rode the crest of each roller, they could see that, although they had the small boat on the appropriate heading to reach the north side of Egmont, the waves and tide were overpowering the force of the wind in their sails. As the boat was pulled farther south, Mike compensated to a more northerly heading, allowing him to narrow the profile of the boat hull against the waves and, at the same time, putting more wind in his sail and increasing his speed.

There was no chaos or tumult, but as the brothers made easterly progress across the channel, the immutable force of the tides and waves silently but swiftly conquered the wind that propelled the boat in the opposite direction and, without saying a word, the passengers knew the goal of crossing the topside of Egmont Key was beyond reach.

Mike continued to adjust his course heading to compensate for the forces of the water and was almost on a beam reach headed north by northeast before they finally made it out of the swift channel and into the backwash on the south side of Egmont. With the force of the tides muted, he once again adjusted course, heading toward the eastern tip of Egmont Key. As they left the big rolling waves of the deep channel, they were back into the rough banging chop they had endured for most of the trip, but there was a palpable sense of relief as Mike reached forward, grabbed the bottle of Wild Turkey with one hand, and leaned back with the tiller in his other. The wind was still strong, but now it was manageable, and a soft rain began to fall from the overcast sky for the first time in the day. The brothers had not said a word since the channel crossing began, but now made eye contact, smiled, and broke into a chuckle at what they had just gone through.

John accepted the outreached offer of the bottle and took a mouthful as the rain hit his face. For a moment, it crossed his mind that the rainwater seemed to be washing away everything in the past and the future, leaving him to enjoy the current moment. He silently watched as his younger brother contentedly steered the small boat through the bouncing chop. Within an hour Mike had landed the boat on the eastern tip of the island, and they got out again to casually examine the shallower and less threatening passage over to Anna Maria Island. That was where the Intercoastal system began, and would provide them relative safe passage for the majority of their trip down to the bottom of the state.

The daylight was no longer in their favor. The sun would be setting in half an hour, and the ride across the Southwest Channel would assuredly take longer than that. There was also an ominous squall line behind them in the west, and while they both felt certain they would be able to make it to the safety of Anna Maria Island and the Intercoastal before the squall overtook them, there would not be a large margin for error.

Once again pulling the boat out into water deep

enough that they could both jump in and immediately drop the centerboard, they began the crossing without the stress that had accompanied the shorter trip across Egmont Channel. The chop seemed to have subsided ever so slightly, and there was a sense of routine that may have actually been fatigue settling in as the long day faded away, with the final act having been the vanquishing of Egmont Channel. Mike pulled out the bottle again and, instead of tossing it back after a pull, stashed it in between his legs as he steered an easterly course toward the amber glow and dark shadows of Anna Maria Island.

As the light slowly diminished, that part of the Earth turning its back to the sun, Mike got up and fastened a flashing beacon to the front of the mast. He was feeling the effects of the bourbon as he stood in the small boat, but was happy he had brought the strobe light—one of the few pieces of safety gear he had actually packed—in the expectation that it was one of those things the race inspectors might actually ask to see.

The weariness of the day and the anticipation of reaching an anchoring point, something to eat, and some time to sleep, combined with the rhythmic banging of the waves and the rattle of the rigging, provided a comforting lullaby as both brothers focused their gaze east, the lights of their destination slowly drawing closer. They both heard the slow, distant hum from the south at about the same time, but neither attached enough significance to say anything, or even look for the source of the sound. After a few minutes, however, the volume had grown to a low growl of sufficient proportions to attract their attention. Without saying a word, they scanned the dark southerly horizon for the oncoming boat that contained the powerful engines.

As the sound grew closer, it seemed to be almost honing in on them, and the anxiety level quickly began to amp up to the highest it had been during the entire day. Mike noticed there was absolutely no light from the moon, and the sun had completely set. It suddenly dawned on him that, damn, it was dark as hell out there.

He thought about the warning whistle he had packed as part of his little nighttime navigation kit, but there was little hope of finding it in the time available as the approaching boat seemed to draw a bead on the brothers like a shark to the scent of blood. Mike thought about reversing course, but quickly assessed that it would be futile as, not being able to see the threat, they were just as likely to steer into its path as away from it. As the adrenaline started to flow, Mike tried to suppress the vision of a boat three times the size of his little pram barreling right over the middle of his boat, twin screws shredding the remains of whatever was left behind after being split into halves.

As the roar of the fast-approaching engines grew louder, it became obvious the oncoming boat was operating without the required running lights. Mike asked John to take the beacon off the mast and point it directly in the direction of the oncoming sound in the off chance that the idiot behind the wheel might actually be looking where he was going. But just as John stood up to unfasten the strobe light, the large shadow accompanying the sound fell upon them.

Neither of the brothers could tell exactly what was happening, but it felt as if the demon boat was passing just behind them. Never slowing down, it was impossible to know if they had actually made physical contact with the larger boat, or just suffered the consequences of extreme proximity to the huge wake cast. Regardless, the result was the lifting of the stern of their small boat to the point where it seemed to actually somersault into the night sky and land back down in a peculiar but perfectly upside-down position, with the mast now pointing directly at the bottom of channel seabed.

As he clung to the capsized boat with one hand, Mike conducted a quick assessment of their situation. He had what was likely just a deep bruise on his left hip and, bringing his right hand to his head, felt a large knot with a small cut and maybe some minor bleeding from where his head had smacked something hard as they went head over heels. From what Mike could see in the darkness, John seemed not to have suffered any serious injuries and was similarly hanging onto the other side of the capsized boat. The former contents of the boat were floating all around them, and it was then that Mike had caught sight of the bag with his booze and other assorted party supplies slowly floating away.

John had left no room for doubt when he declined Mike's suggestion to swim out and rescue the booze. Mike allowed himself a moment of self-pity, wishing he had either drunk a lot more, or a lot less. Now, half drunk, and freshly run over in the dark water of the Southwest Channel of Tampa Bay, he had to figure out what to do next. He was unsure how bad the laceration on his head was, but if it was significant, there was the potential to lose consciousness, and the thought briefly crossed his mind that the blood might attract the bull sharks that were fairly common in the channel. They had only the bottom half of their dry suits on when they went overboard and the water and wind were cool, posing the longer term threat of hypothermia. And, of course, neither of them had been wearing their personal flotation device so, while both were good swimmers, there was the potential to simply drown.

The tides should have been pushing them out deeper into the Gulf of Mexico, but Mike could feel the water moving past them and the boat, as if the boat were anchored somehow. He also realized that, even if the main sail sheet was still locked in place, the boat should have come up on its side, rather than remain upside down.

Shouting to get John's attention, Mike signaled that he was going to dive under the boat. John, who was on the downwind side, acknowledged the plan, and would keep an eye out for Mike surfacing on his side. Taking a big breath, Mike dove under the waves, found the wooden mast, and traced it down to the shallow seabed, where it had been buried in the mud. Planting his feet on both sides, he jerked it out of the mud and then let go, both floating back to the surface.

When he hit the surface, the tide had taken Mike ten feet south of the boat. Swimming back was made harder by the fact that the lower half of his "dry" suit was now full of water, and he was half-full of Wild Turkey. The mast of the boat had floated to the surface, and the boat was now on its side, as it and the two brothers started to move with the tide waters down the channel and into the Gulf. Mike now hung onto the same side of the boat as his brother and, although exhausted, smiled and yelled, "Are we having fun now, or what?"

Having caught his breath, Mike jokingly mocked his older brother. "Don't worry, old man. I've got all this, you just sit back and enjoy the ride!" John did smile and asked if Mike was going to right the boat any time soon and, if not, he would like to order some coffee and dessert. Having agreed that Mike would stand on the part of the hull where the centerboard dropped out of the bottom of the boat, and simultaneously pull back on the starboard-side rail, John agreed to swim back under the boat and hopefully catch the boat as it righted and control the righting process. Part of this would include making sure that the sheet for the mainsail was not locked because, if it were, the wind could catch in the sail and flip the boat right back over on top of Mike or, even worse, simply take off by itself, leaving the brothers in its wake.

Mike started rocking the small boat and the waves finally allowed enough wind to get under the sail that the boat quickly righted herself. Looking at each other on opposite sides of the boat again, John held up his hand

and did a finger countdown of 3 - 2 -1, at which point both of them scrambled over their respective sides and lay on their backs in the small boat.

Sitting up, Mike could still see the lights of Anna Maria Island, but they had lost significant ground as the boat moved south with the tides. There was little moonlight, but, feeling his way around, Mike could tell the back part of the mast mount had been cracked, and the small boom of the main sail had been busted in half. Amazingly, both of the stowed oars were still in place, and Mike pulled them out and locked them into rowing position. Turning the boat eastward, he began rowing and, for the first time since they started the race, felt the accumulated fatigue of the day. The chop of the water made it hard to get a natural rhythm but Mike persisted, rejecting John's insistence to take a turn at the oars.

While they had no clue what time it was, at about 2300 hours they finally reached land somewhere near Anna Maria Island and pulled the boat up onto the beach. It appeared to be a public park area, and, pulling their dry suits off, they walked up to a deserted cement pad, found a water fountain where they both took on a belly full of water, and then passed out on a picnic table.

III

Mike Kelly had started his professional law enforcement career every bit as auspiciously as his older brother, John, had started his military career. Mike had graduated from the Criminal Justice program at Florida State University and quickly started working as a Deputy with Hillsborough County Sheriff's department, the largest such department in western Florida. After completing his probation period, he turned his sights back to school and completed his Master's Degree in Criminal Justice Administration at the University of South Florida in Tampa.

He enjoyed police work, and despite the bureaucracy and politics associated with every sheriff's department in Florida, he clung to the daily proof that his efforts genuinely helped to protect the public and serve justice to those who had done wrong. He developed a reputation as a hard worker, willing to put in uncompensated hours, willing to take risks when needed, and compiling an above-average arrest record.

In Florida, there is one premier law enforcement organization, and, after three years of service with Hillsborough County, Mike was selected for employment as a Special Agent with the Florida Department of Law Enforcement, also known as FDLE. He moved to Miami and quickly became immersed in more complicated investigations. While the targets of his investigations were bigger and more significant, the results were frequently less tangible. He was partnered with a more experienced Special Agent, or SA as they were known in law enforcement jargon, and lost the ability to control the pace of the investigation. Cases frequently dragged on for years, and the influence of the State Attorney became much more important, regularly resulting in the termination of an investigation simply because the Assistant State Attorney had projected that it was not a foregone conclusion they would be able to win a prosecution, and losing cases was not good for a State Attorney's political career.

Mike had worked particularly hard on an investigation of several "boiler rooms" in northern Miami that were selling bogus investments over the phone to unsuspecting victims all across the country. While not a violent crime, Mike had been moved by some the victims' complaints; honest, hardworking folks who had put their entire retirement savings into the hands of a scumbag with a good telephone voice and a convincing script. While the investigation was never popular with his supervisors, Mike had won permission to work undercover at what he considered to be the slimiest of the boiler rooms. Using the leverage of a righteous drug arrest, Mike got one of the employees to vouch for him, and was able to work undercover for three weeks.

While he thought he was well prepared for the undercover assignment, he was in fact overwhelmed by the level of greed that permeated every facet of the operation. Operators sat in small cubicles reading from a script, each phone equipped with a "confidencer" so the intended target could not hear the identical sales pitch being spoken by the other dozen employees working in the room. This particular boiler room was selling worthless "limited partnerships," ostensibly pursuing oil production on land leases from the Federal Bureau of Land Management. It was a classic confidence game, and the slimeballs used every tool at their disposal to dupe the target into thinking it was a genuine business opportunity. There were slick partnership agreements, and prospectuses printed on high-quality paper, subtly implying that the activity had been sanctioned by the BLM.

There were scripts to be read directly by the operators at each phase of the targeting process, including answers for virtually every question a potential target might raise anywhere along the line. Looking through the script, Mike thought to himself that, if you did anything long enough, eventually you were going to hear all the questions there were to ask. These guys had taken the effort of writing the questions down, along with answers. But you weren't required to memorize the questions nor the answers; the pit boss, who was in charge of the room for a given shift, would listen to the phone calls of new employees via an external speaker sitting on every desk and provide the answer. When the victim posed a question, the pit boss would speak the answer right out loud, as though he were talking directly to the target, and the new operators quickly learned to repeat whatever he had said, word-for-word, eventually coming to believe that the confidencers actually worked; the victim could not detect what was going on, and the process actually worked.

In his first evening on the job, Mike made hundreds of phone calls based on information from lead cards, small cards bearing the target's name, address, and phone number. He read from the prepared script while the pit boss, a large and sweaty man with a short temper and a strong liking for gold jewelry and cocaine, hovered next to him with the remote speaker held close to his ear. Mike was taught to push aggressively onward with the initial script, generally talking over any initial objections that might be raised by the target. The goal of this first call was simply to get the target to generally agree to allow the operator to send out one of the new and fancy prospectuses. It was monkey work, but, as he ground through the hours of his shift, which went from 1:00-11:00 pm, he regularly heard other operators ringing bells, indicating they had closed another sale and business was good.

It was during the subsequent follow-up phone calls,

approximately a week after the prospectus package had been sent, that operators defined themselves as winners or losers. And it was in these calls that the pit boss became much more interested, as he got a percentage of every sale. During these calls, another script was read, but the victim, or client/investor as they were referred to on the phone, was allowed to ask more questions. This was the crux of the operation, the good operators were able to immediately provide answers that inspired confidence and cultivated both a sense of greed and urgency within the target. Echoing the word-for-word response of the hovering pit boss was awkward at first, but the operators soon learned that the process worked, and, once the money started to roll in, the good operators were able to answer the questions without any help.

Mike still recalled his first sale, a small-town judge in Indiana. He remembered expressing his logical fear of defrauding a government official such as a judge, and Steve, the fat pit boss, explaining that such government officials were the best targets of all. They often had an arrogance and over-confidence, he explained, that was easily exploited when they were offered an opportunity for quick returns. And when they realized they had been burned, they were the least likely to publicly admit they had been fooled in a swindle.

Mike vividly recalled the judge asking if Mike could guarantee the nineteen percent annual return suggested in the prospectus, and echoing Steve's words in response to the question. "Judge, I can't guarantee the sun is going to come up tomorrow. But I've seen it happen every day of my life, just like I've seen these partnerships double every investor's money for the past five years. So the question isn't whether you're going to get the rate we've been getting; it's whether you want to be in this partnership … or do I give the opportunity to someone else?"

It was a huge money-making machine, with bells ringing every time a sale had been concluded over the phone. The optimal goal was an investment of $100,000, but terms could be negotiated for lower partnership shares, all the way down to $5,000, if that was all the victim could lay his hands on.

When the checks rolled in, they were immediately cashed, and the operators received their twenty-five percent commission at the end of the week. Anyone who obtained an "investor's" agreement to send in a check of more than $30,000 received a gold krugerrand coin on the spot, regardless of what money finally came in. The operation included a break room with endless coffee, and the big earners only had to shout when they wanted something to eat. The pit boss would send one of the new guys out with some cash to fetch the food. It didn't take Mike long to learn that cocaine was regularly used in the break room, although he never did figure out if this was supplied like the coffee, or the operators had to bring their own.

Steve was skilled at keeping the operation working at a feverish pace. "What's the matter, new guy? You getting a little tired? Voice a little worn out? You want some vagisil, you little pussy, or do you want to make some serious money?" It was an artificial pace, but it kept everyone plowing through the cold calls. And there was indeed serious money to be made. Someone would ring a bell and then jump up and begin high-fiving everyone around him, running around the floor, sometimes shouting the amount of commission they had just earned. The more experienced operators would high-five the winner without ever breaking stride in their sales pitch, while the newer guys would hunch over their phones, afraid that the hollering would somehow be heard over the confidencer.

Money was the complete focus. The experienced operators were walking proof that good money could be made, but there was a sense that the good times wouldn't last long. You had to be aggressive and get yours while the getting was good. And inevitably, every conversation or comment regarding a successful sale involved an accompanying derogatory comment about the investor/victim. "Fucking idiot, this guy is actually a Ph.D. teaching college kids biology ... soon he'll be able to give 'em a lesson in economics, dumb motherfucker."

It was always hard and cold, and Mike figured it had to be that way. All the operators knew the investments were bullshit, but it was good money and you did what you had to do to pay the bills. Making the victims out to be chumps, putting the blame for upcoming financial losses on the victim's own shoulders... it was only human nature. It made it easier to make that next sale, bring home the bacon, feel like a winner, and avoid the stress that might come with any deeper reflection.

The longer Mike stayed in the job, the more he also realized the victims did often have to share part of the blame. There were many potential investors who harkened back to what they had been taught since childhood about things that "sounded too good to be true," and they simply hung up on Mike and his fellow operators. Sure, there was the occasional victim who was incompetent to make any significant financial decision about their future, but many more were well-educated, fully capable of accumulating and appropriately investing wealth; they had simply been tempted by greed, by the thought of a quick profit, a little something more than their due. They were not evil for wanting to make a quick profit, but they were also not that different from the operators who lured them into the scam.

The lust for money was at a level Mike had never encountered before. The individual salesmen could make over $100k in the typical six to nine months that a given operation was active. The overhead would seem to be minimal: coffee, pizza, maybe some cocaine for extra encouragement, and the electricity, phone lines, and rent in a relatively safe but dumpy out-of-the-way business park. Mike estimated the sponsors probably made over a million dollars of profit for every three months of operation.

Mike was not without talent, and Steve had spotted it quickly. Mike had a confident delivery, a good voice, and the ability to convey a sense of urgency without ever seeming to care whether this potential client made an investment or not. Steve had taken Mike aside, put his hairy arm around Mike's shoulder, and opined that Mike was a natural. "Stick with me, kid; this is just the tip of the iceberg. You're gonna make good money here, but believe me, you got room to grow. There are opportunities down the road that you can't even imagine. Did you know that I own a forty-five-foot yacht? Don't owe a cent on the bitch, completely paid off. You landed up in the right place; just listen to me, do what you're told, don't think about nothing else, and you will be a rich man very soon."

By the third week of working undercover, checks were starting to roll in from Mike's "clients," and he was the new up-and-comer in the boiler room. During his routine morning briefings at FDLE, however, his bosses and the Assistant State Attorney began to realize the liability involved if people lost their money directly as a result of the sales efforts of an undercover FDLE Special Agent. Warrants were quickly prepared, and a civil cease-and-desist order drafted that would freeze all the funds currently in the operation's bank accounts—hopefully before any of the checks from Mike's clients were cashed.

Mike was disappointed by the hurried and half-assed nature of the actions, but he understood the political realities and went without sleep for thirty-two hours to help prepare the appropriate documents. The bank accounts were frozen, the boiler room was raided, the phone equipment and records were seized, and three operators were arrested on the spot for possession of cocaine.

The following week, without asking anyone, he began to sift through the evidence: shoddy sales records and banking documents to which he had not had prior access, but which confirmed his projections regarding the significant sums of cash that were being generated by the boiler room operation. While the true identity of the individuals actually involved in working the operation had already been confirmed, Mike wanted to dig through the next layer and discover who had financed it, and who was likely, even now, planning the scam that Steve had promised was next in line.

As he started to draft the subpoenas and search warrants that would be the logical next step of the investigation, the quiet mumbling disapproval of his supervisors grew into a bigger obstacle. The boiler room had been shut down; it was an effective disruption operation, and some of the victims would get their money back, but the Department did not have the resources to pursue every crime that occurred in the state of Florida. It was a matter of priorities, and although the boiler rooms were admittedly a rampant problem, especially in south Florida, they were not high on the list of FDLE's objectives. Mike responded by indicating he would do the investigation on his own time and, noting his suspicion that the funding and origin of these operations likely had a few experienced sponsors, identify and prosecute these individuals and it could have an exponential impact on the overall scam industry.

Mike's supervisors at FDLE were sympathetic, but also discreetly explained the realities of the politics involved. The Department had gotten some good press from the arrests and raids, but the anticipated pay off from the next step was likely to be very low in comparison to the work hours he, and others, would inevitably have to dedicate. While they weren't thrilled with the situation, it was what it was; the Department wanted big drug arrests and the takedown of corrupt officials that brought them headlines in the newspapers. The sooner he accepted this, the happier he would be in the long run.

Almost as an act of sympathy, Mike's supervisor agreed with the request that Mike and his partner talk with the Assistant State Attorney (ASA) that had handled the case so far. The ASA, a quick-witted and friendly attorney from New York named Fred, was always receptive and friendly with Mike. He had been a strong supporter of the case, and was happy to have supported the raid that resulted in several arrests and some good headlines.

As soon as Mike and his partner came in, Fred reiterated his congratulations, noting it was the first such takedown of a boiler room in South Florida, and his supervisors were pleased by the case. It was also noted that plea bargains were likely on the drug-related arrests, adding to the always important successful prosecution statistics, and there was no indication anyone from the operation was going to contest what had been seized, yet another favorable development for the case.

Fred noted, however, that he had briefly reviewed the

prospectus and partnership agreements, and, while he agreed the entire deal was a straight-up scam, there was little misrepresentation made in the written documents that could serve as overwhelming proof of intent to commit fraud. And while Mike had worn a wire while working undercover, and the conversations revealed disgusting and deceptive sales practices, they hadn't thought to record the other end of the phone conversations that would be needed to present the open-and-shut case standards typically needed for the current State Attorney to pursue prosecution.

The bottom line, Fred explained, was that the State Attorney was very happy with the case. There had been some good PR generated by the raid, more plea bargains were likely on felony charges, the stats were quick and good, and one set of bad guys had been put out of business.

When Mike made his case to dig deeper into the case, to identify and prosecute the deep pockets that he believed were behind not only this operation, but other operations that popped up like whack-a-moles throughout the state, Fred tried to conceal his lack of interest. He noted that it was one thing to shut down a group of bad guys, but the time and complexities involved in establishing what would likely wind up being a racketeering case, with an unknown probability for success, were clearly not in line with his personal agenda for advancement within the State Attorney's office.

Fred was polite, sympathetic, and genuinely friendly.

He was also honest and made it clear his Office was not likely to invest any more time or resources into the investigation, and this included pursuing any charges beyond those that had already been levied. As consolation, Fred emphasized that FDLE was free to pursue whatever investigation they wanted, but they both knew it was a dead issue.

Mike would have liked to imagine there was some type of omnipotent and conspiratorial corruption working behind the scenes to stymie his investigation into the deep pockets of the boiler room industry; an evil force with which he could do inspired battle, a case of good versus evil. But in truth, he knew it was just the sad compromise of bureaucratic realities. Politicians needed good PR to get elected, prosecutors needed convictions, the Department needed metrics to justify their budget, and little by little, the goal of being the "good guy" was slowly usurped by the goal of getting by.

IV

Mike woke up on top of the beach park table where he had fallen asleep after having landed the boat the prior evening. A stray dog slept peacefully underneath the table as John walked up in the pre-dawn darkness with a ridiculous smile on his face and the smell of hot coffee somehow hovering around him.

"Top of the morning, Skipper" John said softly. Mike was not sure if his brother was mocking him or just in a particularly good mood after having survived the prior evening's misadventure. He sat up and accepted the greeting without response, surveying his surroundings as well as himself. He was stiff and sore, but the lump on the side of his head had subsided and all his extremities seemed to be functioning. He breathed in the coffee aroma, imagining the flavor and comforting warmth as it slid down his parched throat. Despite the aches and pains, the soreness and the salt, Mike looked out beyond the dark beach, listening to the waves roll in, and could not help but think that yes, maybe his brother was right, and it was going to be a fine morning.

Mike stood up and was quickly reminded of the deep bruise he had suffered on his thigh. He looked up toward the beach road and wondered how much time they had before the sun would be up and their privacy would be lost to the light of day.

"There are public showers about 100 yards up the beach. I rinsed out both of our dry suits; they're stretched out over the boat. We'll have to wait till daylight to really know what damage there is to the boat, but it doesn't look like anything serious."

"Senor," Mike responded in a nouveau riche accent, "I don't know anything about this boat of which you speak. This coffee, however, was particularly delicious. Now, I think I will avail of the showers at my personal cabana and, if you would be so kind, I would like a mimosa when I return. And please, use only fresh squeezed oranges … the preservatives in the frozen stuff are not good for my skin."

"Si, Senora. And perhaps some fresh fruit and a massage when you get back?" John played along with his overdone Spanish accent. Mike said nothing and walked creakingly toward the public shower stall, where the water was neither hot nor cold, but soothing as it washed the salt off his aching body.

As he walked back to the park table after his shower, the gulls were starting to squawk and dawn was just starting to break. The brothers walked down to the beach where they had beached the small boat in the early morning darkness. There was enough light now to begin a damage assessment and inventory, and both were surprised at the minimal amount of damage that had been done to the sturdy little boat. The mast collar, which held the bottom of the mast in the boat, had been busted out on the rear side, but this was a minor repair that could easily be accomplished with some new wood, a few screws, and some caulking. The small sail boom had been busted in half, and Mike reached for the side of his head, wondering if the two were connected. But again, this would be a relatively easy repair, requiring only some type of bonding material and a length of locally procured 2x2, or even a discarded broom handle if necessary.

As for the equipment inventory, well, a lot of it was gone. Most significantly, from Mike's perspective, his booze and the bag of weed he had never even gotten to try. The most important item, however, his wallet, was still in the water-tight bag along with a few other essentials, securely fastened under the bow plank. John commented that the damn food Mike had packed, military grade MREs, or "Meals ready to eat", had somehow survived, but they would need to get some water containers ... unless, that was, Mike had decided to switch to an all-alcohol diet.

Tucking his wallet into his shorts, the boys headed back up the beach and into the town of Anna Maria. It was early morning on a Sunday in March, in a small, sleepy tourist town that had not yet swollen to accommodate the crowds that would come with the summer, and this particular morning, the streets were quiet and innocent like a sleeping baby. There were still locals in residence, however, and the boys soon found signs of life stirring at a local breakfast/lunch eatery called Tammy's just a few blocks off the beach. It looked like it might have been a Dairy Queen a few decades prior but, with its location outside the prime beachfront hub of activity, it now looked like the kind of joint that the year-round residents frequented and tried to keep secret from the tourists.

The lights were on inside the restaurant, and the boys could see the shadows of people stirring in the back kitchen, but the doors were locked and the joint was obviously not yet open for business. They sat on the cement steps without saying a word, breathing in the breeze that was just starting to come in off the water, stirring softly as the sun began to warm the land, giving an upward lift to the air, constantly replaced by more of the salty breath until the temperatures ultimately reach a point of homeostasis later in the day.

They were startled as the doors to the restaurant opened up behind them and a hard, wrinkly, yet somehow friendly woman spoke to them. "We don't open for another half hour … but you look a little rough, and I ain't sure you're gonna make it that long." She eyed the ship-wrecked brothers up and down and asked, "You got money to pay … or need a free handout?"

Mike responded by pulling out his wallet. "Yes ma'am,

we'd be paying customers. Apologize about how we look but we had some boat problems last night."

"No worries little Jimmie, we don't have a dress code. Come on in, assume you want some coffee?"

"Yes ma'am" replied Mike again, as the old lady headed back to the kitchen, pondering whether she called everyone younger than herself "little Jimmie".

Returning to their table with a pot of coffee, she poured the warm brew and asked if they knew what they wanted or needed some time to look at the menus. Asking what she recommended, they ended up ordering grits with shrimp, and a scrambled egg-with-sausage croissant sandwich. In the process, they learned that the old lady's name was Tammy and that she had owned and operated the restaurant for the last fifteen years, never taking a single day off.

"You were just outside," she explained. "It's March and the temperature is sixty degrees before the sun comes up. The breeze has started; I'm done by three each afternoon. I'll see a bunch of old friends come in and out all day. If the tide is running when I ride my bicycle over the bridge on the way back home, I'll probably watch the porpoises feeding. If conditions are right, might even take the skiff out and do some fishing myself. Who needs a day off when my whole life is a vacation?" She didn't wait for a response.

"But it is Sunday, and if you're inclined, St. Patrick's is two more blocks east and mass is at 11:00 during the off-season; you look like it might do ya good ... and they don't have no dress code neither." Tammy chuckled to herself as she headed back to the kitchen.

The boys sat silent for a while before John finally said, "Wow, I'm having a tough time remembering the last time I went to a real Mass." He paused before continuing. "But if you're going to stay at the helm indulging your newly-found bad habits … maybe I ought to heed the wisdom of Ms. Tammy and get things right with the Lord." He chuckled to himself much as Tammy had moments before.

"Very funny," Mike responded, silently recalling that his last time in a church had been for a funeral that rocked the foundation of his life, but unable to recall the last regular Mass he had attended.

"I assume you must have covered your bets while you were over in the Afghanistan. Is it true what they say, that there are no atheists in a foxhole?" Mike asked while stirring the sugar into his coffee.

"You know, it wasn't like the old days and going to a formal Mass when we were kids, but now that you mention it, I did make it to services of one sort or another whenever I got the chance." John paused, clearly reflecting before continuing. "And it did all seem to have a much more immediate relevancy given the circumstances … funny how that happens when you find yourself in the middle of the shit."

"It wasn't always a Catholic Mass, although I did actually look forward to old rituals from our youth when a priest showed up for services. But the whole situation kind of condensed things to a very fine point—kind of added focus or clarity—at least for me. I liked the simplicity of a Mass where the altar was a bunch of crates and everyone wore the same uniform."

"But there were other guys who adamantly refused anything to do with religion. I remember thinking that maybe they were afraid it was a sign of weakness ... or they thought it would distract them from concentrating on the objective of staying alive, which generally involved killing the enemy to the best of your ability." John paused for a while before breaking the silence. "Kiss my ass on the issue of foxholes and atheists, son, you have enough serious issues of your own to ponder sitting here in Ms. Tammy's little paradise in the land of milk and honey."

"True enough," Mike responded, ending the conversation just as Tammy delivered a hot breakfast and more small talk to the table.

"So you said you had some boat trouble last night?" she asked.

"Nothing big really. Got a small sailboat and hit a rough patch out in the dark last night. Need to make a few repairs; we're taking something of a leisure cruise down the Inland Coastal Waterway."

"You aren't one of them knuckleheads I heard about trying to kayak all the way from Tampa down to Key West by any chance, are you?"

"Well, we aren't supposed to admit it, and I've got a small sailboat rather than a kayak, but yes, we're one of the knuckleheads," Mike responded, maybe with a sense of pride at being recognized for his adventurous spirit.

"You sure are slow! A whole bunch of them kayakers passed through here yesterday and got a quick meal before I even closed. And then I saw a whole herd more on my way home going over the bridge. And they didn't even have no sails; they were just plugging away with their oars … mostly looked like real old guys too. Ain't they got any time limit on how long it takes to finish?"

So much for Mike's pride and adventurous spirit. According to Tammy, he was not only slow, but lazy. He almost started to explain the inherent complications of using wind to drive a boat rather than the direct propulsion of paddling; the berth and stability factors designed into sailing craft that resulted in slower speeds in light winds; the fact that they had gotten run over in the middle of the night by some clueless, probably drunk, motor-boater and were lucky to even be alive.

He almost started to explain, but he didn't. "Yea, I guess you could say we're slow" Mike said with a resigned smile. "But like you said, what's the rush, right? We're here in paradise, why hurry out?" But he couldn't resist a final jab. "Besides, my brother built the boat, and it's slower than a swimming cow." Mike desperately wanted to look at this brother and see how much of a reaction he had been able to evoke, but avoided the temptation, dead-panning the line as best he could.

"Ah, don't worry little Jimmie, it was a little rough out there yesterday, especially early on. And I didn't mean to hurt your feelings. You may be younger and stronger than them old guys I saw, but for some reason, I got a feeling you don't have as much to prove as they might. You stay safe..." Tammy paused before adding, "But if you are going back out there, remember Mass is at 11:00; it couldn't hurt." She chuckled to herself again as she put the check on the table.

Mike asked if there was a hardware store in town that might be open, and Tammy provided instructions to a store a few blocks over that would be opening in just about the time it would take to walk there. Mike left a big tip for the very moderately-priced breakfast, and as the two walked out of the empty restaurant, the first regular customers were walking up the steps.

The sun was fully awake as the boys walked over to the hardware store and, just as Tammy had predicted, the store was opening up as they arrived. They threw some wood screws, caulking, a yard of canvass, thread and needle, and a few small lengths of lumber in the handbasket. Neither could remember whether they still had a screwdriver, so they bought one just to be sure. They weren't sure why, but they bought a roll of duct tape—it was so utilitarian you just couldn't have too much duct tape. The hardware fit into one small bag, and the lumber was carried easily over the shoulder as Mike paid with his credit card, glad that it was his habit to keep a zero monthly balance now that he was totally dependent on its available credit.

"You don't happen to know where there is an open liquor store, do you?" Mike asked the cashier as they checked out.

"You have got to be kidding me!" John mumbled as they were walking out, after the clerk had provided directions. "It's Sunday morning! It's barely 09:00! And you're asking after a liquor store? Are you aware that these are indications you have a problem? Are you gonna try to rustle up a weed dealer also, Detective?"

"Wow, that's a little harsh, don't you think?" Mike responded lackadaisically. "First of all, this is Florida, where the use of liquor is promoted by the state 24/7 as evidenced by the very fact that there is a liquor store open at this obscene hour on a Sunday morning. I submit that, if it were not government policy to encourage the consumption of alcoholic beverages this morning, these establishments would not be granted a license to operate during said hours. I prefer to view the purchase as my civic duty … do you know how much tax income the state derives from liquor sales?"

"Further, my inhibited and puritanical brother, I highlight the fact that I am on vacation. While I can't speak authoritatively on the habits of your brethren in military uniform, as a general rule, we in law enforcement tend to indulge the spirits when we are on vacation. While it might be argued that my eager and early consumption on this particular boat trip might be interpreted as an early-warning indicator, I prefer the alternate view that it is a timely, appropriate, and therapeutic response to the afflictions associated with work in the modern world. Besides, we're sailors, and sailors drink."

"And finally, as for your insensitive comments about

the possible consumption of cannabis, I would like to highlight to you that I never even got to touch the insides of the bag ... thank you once again for watching it bob away on the waves, all of about five feet away from you, while you clung to the boat like a scared little girl."

"And no, I do not intend to try to buy some more. While I may exceed your risk tolerance on this free-spirited sailing adventure, I am not foolhardy. Despite your assertions to the contrary, my judgment is impeccable and, as a veteran law enforcement officer with significant experience at the federal, state, and local levels, I am aware that the purchase of illicit substances in an unfamiliar environment is always an extremely dangerous undertaking."

At the liquor store, Mike bought three bottles of Wild Turkey bourbon and a single bottle of Stolichnaya vodka, offering the exaggerated explanation to an uninterested sales clerk that he was setting out on an epic boating adventure, and was not sure when he would next see land, let alone the inside of a liquor store. Mike asked that the bottles be triple wrapped in paper bags to avoid them banging against each other.

They walked back to the boat in silence, Mike only now beginning to understand the depth of the sentiments his brother held regarding the liquor purchases. They had gone through awkward disagreements in the past, and they had both learned there was rarely anything productive that would come out of additional conversation. The situation was what it was, and talking wasn't going to change it.

Besides, despite all the cavalier rhetoric, Mike Kelly was well aware of his problems and the downward spiral he had been on for the last several months. But that was what the trip was all about, right? The sun had come up this morning, he was still alive, hope sprang eternal; sometimes whether you wanted it to or not. Mike didn't mention that, in the back of his mind, he had been thinking about going to Mass ever since they left Tammy's.

By the time they had efficiently made repairs to the mast collar and the boom, re-filled the water jugs, and stashed the liquor below the bow plank, it was approaching the middle of the day and the temperature was warm. Their first conversation of substance since leaving the liquor store was whether to wear their dry suits. The weather was fine and conditions looked fair but, as they had learned the prior evening, things could change quickly. Despite the warmth of the beach, it was still March, and if they were tossed overboard, the water was cold and hypothermia would soon become a very real concern. The boat was too small to put the dry suits on while they were out on the water, so it was agreed they would put the suits on, but leave the top half unzipped and hanging from their hips in order to prevent overheating. They both wore special-blend long-sleeved white T-shirts that protected against sunburn, and were also good at wicking sweat away from the body.

They pulled the boat down to the water's edge and John did a final walk-around, looking for any damage they might have missed earlier in the morning. The wind was blowing inland from the west and Mike suggested the obvious, that they row out past the breakers, and then head due south along the coast of the island. The initial plan had been to go on the inside of Anna Maria Island, sailing on the more gentle water of the Inland Coastal Waterway, or ICW as it was known in boating shorthand. But the mishap of the prior evening had resulted in their beaching on the western, outer side of the island, which faced the Gulf of Mexico, and the possibility of backtracking up to the northern end of the island just to get into the ICW was never even mentioned. Neither really considered themselves genuine competitors in the EcoLoco Challenge, but they had been on the water enough throughout their lives that they had no inherent fear of the Gulf of Mexico. It would be a challenging sail, but as long as the wind and waves didn't pick up too much, they would be able to make good time sailing at a 90-degree angle to the wind. The plan was to keep the shore in sight and, in another nine miles or so, they would be able to see the opening of Longboat Pass, where they could enter into the relative safety of Sarasota Bay, and get back in line with the kayakers who had apparently forged the more efficient path many hours prior.

The boys experienced no problems getting off the beach, sailing southwest until they were approximately 300 yards off shore. The water was still shallow, maybe nine feet, and the waves were mild and rolling as the boat turned more directly toward the south. No longer plowing through the waves at an angle, but sailing parallel to them, made for a significant side-to-side rolling of the type that frequently prompted sea sickness in new sailors, but it wasn't bothering either of the boys this morning. There was regular wash-over into the boat, but that was easily handled with the bail bucket and, all things considered, both brothers quickly began to relax, settling into their habits and enjoying the quiet sea and sun. Lost in their own thoughts, Mike wondered at the human condition, and how the events of the prior evening, and even the friction of a few hours earlier, could so quickly and easily be washed away in the rocking contentment of the tiny boat. He pulled one of the jugs of water out from below the mid-plank and took a long drink before silently passing it to his brother. John accepted without a word being spoken, took a similar long drink, and left the jug out on the floor of the boat between the two.

V

While Mike Kelly had been frustrated with what he considered to be the unsatisfying conclusion to the boiler room investigation in North Miami, he did not let his frustration show, and continued pursuit of other cases with an unrelenting enthusiasm and aggressiveness. He eagerly learned about narcotics investigations, playing a supporting role on several important cases that resulted in the prosecution of some regional dealers. His heart, however, was not invested in the cases and, in truth, he felt the war-on-drugs was unwinnable using traditional law enforcement methods.

While most of the Special Agents working on the drug task force were drawn to the traditional targets of marijuana, cocaine, and heroin networks that seemed to inevitably originate from one Latin American country or the other, Mike found himself once again veering from the main stream and taking the lead in working against the growing population of "pain clinics" that seemed to be popping up on virtually every street corner of South Florida. There had been no hue and outcry against these clinics and, although it would eventually become a favorite topic of politicians and the media, at the time, Mike was the only one sounding the alarm.

Based on information from a source who had been arrested for heroin distribution and was looking to minimize his jail term, Mike learned about the pernicious qualities of prescription drugs like Oxycodone and Oxycontin that were liberally distributed from the pain clinics under the cover of genuine medical practice. Synthesized from the same poppy plant that produces heroin, Oxycodone was first developed in 1916 with the initial and noble intent of helping those in great pain, primarily wounded soldiers in battle. He learned how these synthetic drugs had been tailored to mimic the pain relief provided by opiate treatments like morphine, but with fewer of the side effects such as nausea. While the initial intent included hopes that the drug would be less addictive, advancements in chemical science ironically produced a product that could be used more often, with more focused intensity and fewer side effects, and eventually landed up being even more addictive than heroin in the long run.

As with morphine, the use of Oxycodone had quickly been subverted by those suffering from emotional or mental ailments for which it was never intended. The Oxycontin version provided a time-released tablet that made it possible to experience the effects without the use being readily apparent to anyone other than the user. But regardless the method or brand name, it quickly became a spiderweb from which there was no easy escape. Those abusing the drug had been drawn to its numbing effect as a result of psychological or emotional injuries, and the drugs only compounded and buried the root cause of the problem deeper into the abyss. The escape provided by the drug eventually and inevitably made it the overriding object of desire in the user's life and, much like heroin years before, diminished the apparent value of everything else in the user's life.

What had captured Mike's intense interest was that, unlike other drug abuse schemes that law enforcement typically prosecuted, Oxycodone was openly marketed and promoted under the cover of legitimate health management. As a kid, Mike had heard grown-ups talk about "pushers" of marijuana, dealers who offered unsuspecting youths free marijuana in an attempt to get them "hooked", a practice authorities warned would inevitably lead to a life of crime and destitution while lining the pockets of the dealers. Mike had never actually seen this dynamic in action at the time.

But now, despite an awareness that his comments sounded like a 1960s government warning movie trailer, he had absolutely no doubt that the pain clinics spreading through South Florida were acting as the "pushers" his elders had warned him about many years ago. Although they were in no way the innocent flowers of youth portrayed in the '60s government propaganda, users would wander into one of these clinics and complain of chronic pain of one sort or the other, and would inevitably walk out with a prescription for Oxycodone. Typically, they would save some for their own use, and sell the balance of the prescription to others who were further down the road of addiction. The whole enterprise operated out in the open, under the cover of legitimate medicine, and, while the media and establishment would eventually awaken to the growing epidemic, at the time, Mike felt very alone in his outrage over the legal distribution of these drugs.

As he looked closer at the illicit industry, he began to uncover the attributes of a traditional organized crime industry. Principals would open up "clinics" in strip malls, he estimated at the rate of one every week, and would hire a physician typically trained abroad and who held little hope of being successful with a mainstream medical practice. All they had to do was hang a sign from the roof bearing the words *pain management*, and the clients would begin showing up on an ever-increasing basis.

The enterprises varied in how much they tried to cover what they were doing. Some would dispense prescriptions based on nothing more than a complaint of an old back injury, while the more sophisticated would require the patient to get an X-ray or an MRI, which could inevitably be interpreted as showing some symptoms of arthritis or some other anomaly that ostensibly could be causing pain to justify the issuance of the prescription.

The more Mike investigated the initial comments of his source, the more he realized that the size and scope of the problem was completely overwhelming. He had verified reports from his source that groups were traveling into South Florida from other states to visit the clinics and immediately returning home to distribute the pills, which typically sold for twenty to thirty dollars per pill, depending on where they eventually got re-sold. A drive through the parking lot in front of any one of these pain clinics would inevitably reveal at least a few license plates from Kentucky and Ohio, although Mike was not sure how or why these states were so connected with the distribution schemes.

He had initially brought his concerns to one of the Supervisory Special Agents on the Counter-Narcotics Task Force (CNTF) and, while he listened patiently, it was clear he thought of the issue as a second-rate threat involving relatively safe prescription drug abuse, not the epidemic Mike was describing. Despite his doubt however, he agreed to allow Mike to discuss the issues with the Assistant State Attorney, or ASA, who was working exclusively on CNTF cases.

The ASA handling CNTF cases for Dade County was Ricardo Blanchard, a young, aggressive, and charismatic Cuban who would eventually enter politics and do very well. He was hard-working and well-intentioned, and intrigued by Mike's reporting on the alleged epidemic of Oxycodone abuse, and the network of pain clinics that served as a distribution network. As Mike relayed his initial findings, Blanchard immediately recalled half a dozen pain clinics that he passed every day on his way to and from his office in downtown Miami, but he had never stopped to wonder what the hell was going on. Although he had never heard anyone else speak about the scope of the problems Mike was reporting, Blanchard found every aspect of Mike's reporting credible. And the passion in Mike's voice when he talked about what he was uncovering could not help but stir the dust off some of those loftier goals Blanchard had held when he first applied to law school. And the more he thought about it, the more Ricardo's mind turned to the question of whether this could be an opportunity to make a name for himself, a chance to finally boost himself into the big leagues of politics.

Very quickly, Ricardo Blanchard became one of Mike's biggest fans, but he insisted on keeping the investigation very low profile and was reluctant to bring in additional investigators. Mike was initially tasked with identifying the networks inside of the pain clinic industry, which was, if the pain clinics were connected to each other, a task that involved numbing but non-alerting research through public databases such as business licenses and incorporation documents. The work was done concurrent with Mike's more traditional investigatory work, and he did not tell his coworkers or his supervisors about his activities with Blanchard. It took approximately six months to uncover what he thought were three large networks, each consisting of at least twenty multiple pain clinics in South Florida. He had sent his source into several clinics from each of the networks, and it was confirmed that there were operational commonalities across facilities of each network that seemed to bind them together, and also served to differentiate them from the other networks. One of the most obvious connections was that many of the facilities within a given network would have the same physician, who would travel from one office to the other on different days of the week, making it easier for those who had lost all their worldly belongings to the effects of the addiction, to simply walk in and obtain some more, rather than have to endure the arduous bus ride across town. It also appeared that the networks shared cultural bonds; one seemed to employ primarily Pakistani/Indian medical professionals, while another seemed to favor medical professionals from Laos and China.

Nine months after their initial meeting, with three apparent major networks mapped out, Blanchard took the first of his official actions on the case, issuing subpoenas for the banking records associated with the networks. At the same time, he opened the case up a little further by meeting with the regulatory side of the Drug Enforcement Administration. While the DEA was most well-known for the Special Agents that kicked down doors and captured drug lords overseas, a larger portion of the Agency's budget was actually spent on regulatory activities, and these regulations could be a treasure trove of information for anyone investigating the illicit distribution of Class II controlled substances.

Of course, a State prosecutor making inquiry of a

federal agency like the DEA frequently provoked more questions than positive results, and it was no different in this case. Shortly after making the inquiry, Blanchard was visited by one of the DEA Supervisory Special Agents assigned to the CNTF who was not shy in asking about the background of Blanchard's inquiry and politely noting that things would likely be better received if Blanchard had routed such a request through the Agents assigned to the CNTF. Blanchard feigned an apology and explained his recent receipt of reports indicating the existence in South Florida of networks using licensed physicians to distribute synthetic opiates; Blanchard deliberately avoided mentioning Mike's involvement in the investigation.

Upon receipt of the briefing, the senior DEA Agent almost immediately lost interest but agreed to support Blanchard's request. "Good luck with that..." was his exact response once he realized that the investigation involved licensed physicians. Beyond the fact that such investigations simply lacked the adrenaline potential of more traditional drug investigations, the Agent made reference to an incredible number of hurdles deliberately built into the bureaucracy and specifically designed to protect physicians from the second-guessing inquiries of perceived gun-toting, unsophisticated Special Agents.

There were already more classic drug distribution cases than the Task Force could handle; cases involving tons of heroin and marijuana imported from abroad, many involving terrorist connections. These cases were easier to prosecute, the Agents were more familiar and comfortable with the investigative tools and, at the end of the day, such cases produced the ever-persistent demand for metrics that drove both personal promotion and organizational budgets. The Agent admitted he was aware of a rapid increase in the trafficking of Oxycodone, and even reports of exponential price increases due to demand, but explained that it was an issue that lacked political legs. Pursuit of a bunch of foreign doctors, with minimal expectation of successful prosecution, was simply not something the Agent wanted to invest his career potential in. If Blanchard had the time and interest, the Agent wished him the best of luck, indicating he would help where possible.

The first trove of prescription issuance records arrived at Blanchard's office about three months after the initial request. Mike had been called in by an excited Blanchard to look at the histories of the physicians identified within the networks. The documents, in and by themselves, seemed so compelling it was hard to imagine anything but an easy prosecution. Blanchard had the forethought when he made the initial request to also ask for comparisons against which he could gauge the activities of the pain clinics under investigation. It turned out that every one of the physicians under investigation exceeded the national average issuance of Oxycodone prescriptions by at least twenty-fold. As they sat in the office, Blanchard smugly commented that, if his understanding of the reporting was correct, the physicians Mike had identified were the most prolific scrip writers for opiates in the entire country. In fact, Blanchard noted with incredulity, it seemed almost every one of them had individually issued more scrips for Oxycodone than all the other doctors outside of Florida … combined.

It was an "Ah-hah" moment of silent satisfaction. The proverbial smoking gun lay in front of them in black-and-white, indisputable statistics. They, on their own, had identified a true scourge of society. They, alone, had persevered where others had relented, and had found the proof of a growing epidemic.

Nine months later, the bloom of enthusiasm had faded to cold gray as Blanchard slowly came to appreciate the prosecutorial complexities and obstacles forewarned by the DEA Supervisory Special Agent. While civil lawsuits alleging malpractice could have been won easily based on the evidence available, there were not likely to be any such lawsuits where the ostensible "patients" were in practical collusion with the physicians who were feeding their addiction. And criminal prosecution of the physicians required a much higher threshold, essentially requiring the prosecutor to demonstrate the same level of apparent intent on the part of the physician as that of a trafficker who concealed bales of marijuana on a fast boat and secretly unloaded them on US shores under cover of darkness.

The Controlled Substances Act regulated the dispensing of drugs like Oxycodone, but left an enormous amount of wiggle room for any competent defense attorney. The regulation's amorphous wording specified that prescriptions could only be issued for "legitimate medical purpose" by an authorized medical professional within the usual course of professional practice. Establishing that the involved physicians had deliberately issued prescriptions beyond the medicinal needs of their patients was a very difficult threshold to cross.

Research into relevant case law had established that many of the practices employed by the suspect physicians would effectively mitigate any prosecutorial efforts. The mere act of performing a quick medical examination, or requiring an X-ray, however inconclusive it might turn out to be, served to establish an adequate defense that the physician was pursuing the patient's medical needs. And even in the absence of these acts, prior prosecution of physicians had generally required some additional act to indicate positive intent, such as warning the patient not to fill multiple prescriptions at the same pharmacy, or deliberately misdating multiple prescriptions to the same patient.

Everything that had been collected in Mike's investigation thus far indicated that the physicians in the South Florida networks had paid close attention to prior case law, and had taken action accordingly. While they had dispensed more Oxycodone than all physicians outside of the state of Florida combined, they appeared to always perform at least a perfunctory physical examination, sometimes even asking for X-rays of a claimed injury. While they could not deny the overwhelming amount of prescriptions they had written for opiates, this would never meet the prosecutorial requirement to prove that they were intentionally distributing the opiates for non-medicinal purposes.

The realizations and disheartening conclusions had been assimilated in a piecemeal manner. Blanchard eventually indicated that the investigation would need to be re-focused on the physicians' income, deducing that they had to be receiving a share of the profits from the prescriptions they wrote. The risks these doctors were taking logically had to be justified by proceeds exceeding the small Medicaid reimbursements they received for seeing the patients. The identification of the as-yet unidentified source of this income, and the associated financial records, would be the missing link that connected the physicians more directly to the drug distribution activities and more firmly establish their criminal intent. But issuing subpoenas for physicians' financial records, no matter their place on the medical hierarchy, was not something that the government undertook lightly. It would be years before a successful prosecution was scored.

In the meantime, Mike had continued his successful career trajectory, enthusiastically accepting an offer to become a Special Agent with the Federal Bureau of Investigation. It was certainly the most significant step in his career and, while he had done his fair share of moaning about prima donna, big-ego, FBI Special Agents while he had worked for County and State law enforcement, he had always secretly wanted to carry the badge that represented the pinnacle of law enforcement, and even more secretly hoped to finally be able to go to sleep at night sated with a sense of accomplishment and satisfaction at the work he had done.

VI

Within a couple of uneventful hours, Mike and John had the boat headed east, with the wind at their back, as they slipped easily through Longboat Pass into the intercoastal waters of Sarasota Bay. They made good time as they then turned almost due south on a close reach, averaging over four knots, passing under the Ringling Causeway and then Siesta Drive Bridge and into the muddy waters of Roberts Bay. It was easy sailing, essentially keeping the Florida mainland on the left, and a series of barrier islands on the right, with an ever-vigilant and distrustful eye out for big boats with motors. By late afternoon they had made it to Little Sarasota Bay. Its abundance of shallows and sandbars, combined with the waning sun, caused them to refocus their attention on navigation, hoping to avoid running aground and damaging their dagger board or rudder.

While this was the second day of the race, and virtually all of the real competitors would have already made it to the first checkpoint just north of Charlotte Harbor, the brothers had quietly agreed while looking at the charts earlier in the morning that they'd be lucky to make it to Venice. What went unsaid was the mutual understanding that they were not competing with anyone else in the race and, given the events of the prior evening, they were both inclined to avoid any night sailing if at all possible.

As the sun began to set, they pulled the boat through some mangroves to the back side of a boat ramp and set up a primitive camp, unseen by the many boaters who were washing their boats before heading home. Mike pulled out two spaghetti MREs, and the boys ate quietly as they watched the last of the boats pack up and leave. A park ranger responsible for locking up the boat ramp was the only one who noticed them and headed in their direction but, half-way there, stopped and turned around without ever saying a word. He locked the gate on his way out, and the boys were alone. They started a small fire and unpacked the small sleeping bags that had somehow survived the capsizing of the prior evening.

Mike, who had consciously avoided drinking during the afternoon to avoid aggravating his brother, pulled out one of the bottles of Wild Turkey and had a few swigs. John refilled the water bottles from the hose at the fish-cleaning table and declined an invitation to share the whiskey when he returned. Mike shrugged, but was glad to see that the reappearance of the bottle didn't seem to vex his brother. *Okay,* he thought, *I guess the rule is, it's okay to drink on dry land during vacation,* but he whispered not a word of the thought to his older brother.

The spaghetti MREs were military grade, and although they inevitably brought back memories of some very difficult situations for John, they tasted good and, being warm, were quickly eaten and well appreciated. No matter how many times Mike made one of these meals, he couldn't stop himself from experiencing some level of awe as he poured water into the heavy duty plastic bags and watched them magically heat the meals to a level that was too hot to hold. It was a model of efficiency, and although they never quite met the threshold of delicious, it was pretty damn efficient for anything associated with the government. And, if you were hungry enough, Mike supposed the meals could quickly slip over the threshold and slide into the category of delicious.

As the evening turned cold, the brothers drew closer to the small fire, sitting cross-legged and staring into the flames as men are wont to do, as if somehow hypnotized by the simple flickering flame. John commented with pleasure on the lack of mosquitoes but Mike did not respond, having another slow pull off the bottle without taking his eyes off the fire.

"Do you think you have PTSD?" Mike asked his brother without explanation, never taking his gaze off the fire's flames.

"I assume so …" John responded without hesitation but also without certitude. "Yeah, probably…"

"What the fuck does that mean? 'Yeah, probably…'? Don't you have to take tests and stuff before you come back to civilization to make sure you're at least mostly squared away?" Mike asked with genuine, if not exactly empathetic, disbelief.

"Always you and the F-word," John retorted. "Don't you have to take some type of test to make sure you have a vocabulary sufficient to write an investigatory report without resorting to the use of profanity?"

Mike was back in the mix with his brother, assuming the voice of so many defense lawyers he had observed over the years. "Nice attempt to misdirect; now, please answer the question: Were you, or were you not, required by the US Military to submit to psychological evaluation subsequent to your latest combat tour; said evaluation being made in an attempt to determine whether you were suffering from Post-Traumatic Stress Disorder and/or other mental/emotional illnesses typically associated with the violence of combat?"

"No sir, I was not required to take any such testing," John responded, playing along as if he were being questioned in court.

"Well, if not required, was such psychological testing and evaluation at least made available to you at the end of your combat tour?"

"Yes sir. The US Army provides for full psychological assessment and treatment of its soldiers at all times, not just at the end of a combat tour. All personnel are encouraged to be alert to the possible negative psychological and emotional consequences of combat, and to take full advantage of the services offered" John responded with a regimental voice of authority that had complete confidence in its ability to break all issues down into matters made either black or white. There were no shades of gray in official policy and the voice knew that, when the shadows of dusk grew long, hiding things known only to those who there at the time, there was sometimes comfort and reassurance to be found in the clarity of military orders and regulations.

"So, you did not avail yourself of these services?"

"No sir, I did not."

"And doesn't that, by logic, dictate that you were probably in need of such treatment and, by extension of the same logic, indicate that you are now probably as crazy as a fucking loon?"

"Sir, I am once again offended by your language."

"I apologize. Now please answer the fucking question."

"No sir, I did not take advantage of the psychological evaluation services offered by the US Government" John answered as Mike sat back with a buzz from the bourbon and a smugness at winning the contest, the ultimate point of which he could no longer remember.

But after only a few seconds of respite, John couldn't stop himself. "You know, since you seem to want to talk about emotional and psychological issues, perhaps you'd like to expand on your current drinking habits and when, exactly, you began your own dance with the demons of night."

It was a long period of silence that followed, somehow empty and yet, at the same time, legion with painful scars, fears, and doubts common to both of these blood brothers, yet never mentioned aloud at night or in the light of day, in accordance with some unknown rule imprinted on their souls at birth.

"Goodnight John-Boy," was Mike's only response, harkening back to the TV show *The Waltons* that they had watched together as kids, surrendering the battle rather than risk broaching all the issues associated with John's question. They had both spent many evenings wrestling with the banshees of the dark, and they each suspected the same specters had visited the other, but to speak of it out loud might give the ghosts an even greater power. Out of fear, the fears themselves were buried deep in the belly.

Mike had a few more pulls off the bottle, and the two fell asleep in the cool of the night.

VII

The brothers awoke peacefully to the sounds of the shorebirds about an hour before dawn. They ate granola bars and drank as much water as they could force themselves to drink as they packed up their bags and stowed their gear back into the small boat. They spread the laminated nautical maps out on the wet camp grass and studied them using a unique form of flashlight that Mike had found on-line: a simple plastic cap that slipped over a 9-volt battery and powered a small but effective LED light that seemed to last forever.

There was not much to talk about. The course for the day was pretty simple and clear. They would enter the man-made Venice Canal and, depending upon the winds, sail or row the following five miles before entering back into the natural ICW at Lemon Bay. They would then sail the following fifteen nautical miles with a little more room to maneuver, including the ability to tack into the wind if needed, but still without much opportunity to make any significant navigational mistakes. At the bottom end of Lemon Bay was Don Pedro Island State Park, the first check-in point of the EcoLoco challenge, where some of the faster boats would have likely passed through at the same time Mike and John were upside down off Ana Maria Island. The check-in post was scheduled to have closed the prior evening, but it was possible there would still be someone there, and the boys agreed they would stop and check, just in case.

Beyond Lemon Bay was an expected easy sail through Placida Harbor and then passage through Charlotte Harbor, a task they both assessed as one of the most potentially dangerous sections of the entire trip. Decisions on how to proceed at that point would depend greatly on the weather and, as there was no way to know what the weather would be like when they got there in the afternoon, further discussion was deferred until they made it through Lemon Bay.

The park warden was opening up the gate to the parking lot as the brothers shipped out and sailed across the front of the boat ramps. As they had assumed, there was little recreational boat traffic now that the weekend had passed. The morning was cold, but the sun was coming up bright. There would have normally been a strong "land breeze," but the steep banks of the Venice Canal conspired to deprive the sailors the benefit of this gentle form of propulsion.

Mike and John agreed to take one-hour shifts rowing, both knowing the other would row until dark before he suggested his turn was up. They wore large wristwatches that served multiple functions, and Mike had teased John about the size and brand of his watch, calling it a "wrist clock." The police forces surrounding Tampa had an abundance of military reserve personnel, many of whom were associated with MacDill Air Force Base, which, sitting in the middle of Tampa Bay, served not only as the home of US Central Command, but also Special Operations Command, both of which had seen more than their fair share of duty during recent wars in Iraq and Afghanistan. Mike had observed that guys coming back from war-zone tours inevitably seemed to all wear the Suunto brand watch his brother was now wearing, an oversized watch made in Finland and reportedly the most useful and reliable when your ass was on the line. Mike would never make fun of a full-time soldier wearing the watch, but a fellow cop coming back from reserve duty, even if he was in the same shit-hole tour of duty as the full-time soldier, somehow seemed fair game. And the same twisted logic also prevailed when it came to teasing his brother.

"I'll take the first turn," Mike had said. "Make sure you've got the sun dials on your wrist clock all lined up so you know when it's your turn."

"You lust for this watch," John had replied, "but you know you can't wear it because it's designed for soldiers, not *Miami Vice* detectives concerned about fashion."

"Oooh, the quiver... it flies true and pierces my core ..." Mike answered with feigned offense. "Just make sure your fancy wrist clock knows when an hour is up and it's time for my nap, soldier boy."

With the lack of wind, the sail was completely trimmed and wrapped vertically along the length of the mast. The oar locks were placed into their mounts and Mike, facing the rear of the small boat and trying to alternate looking over his left and right shoulder to make sure of his course, deftly pulled the two eight-foot oars through the smooth surface of the Venice Canal. John leaned back in the bow of the small boat, silently admiring the skill evident in his brother's rowing technique, knowing that it was not near as easy as Mike made it look. The sun was now stretching out and, with the lack of any breeze, the chill of the prior evening was evaporating and it would soon be warm. Both brothers were wearing full dry suits, which zipped up the front and were designed to keep out all water, even if fully immersed. But they also held in incredible amounts of heat, and both had once again unzipped the suits and pulled off the upper half to let the body heat escape.

They had both retained most of their personal gear after the capsizing on Tampa Bay and, while the first issue was protecting themselves from potential hypothermia associated with the March waters, a close second was protection from the sun. John still had a floppy cotton hat he had brought back from Afghanistan, which had served him well in the desert heat but was slow to dry out once wet. Mike's hat was one of the things he had lost in the darkness of the capsizing. It was an expensive piece of equipment, and one of the few things he had really given much thought to in preparation for the adventure. It was made of special nylon blend that was light, flexible, quick-drying, and included some sort of built-in U.V. sunscreen material. It even had a flap that could be rolled down and protected the neck from sunburn. In its absence, he had bought an over-sized straw tourist hat in Ana Maria and, despite its low-tech qualities, he had become quite enamored with it, believing that it did a better job of allowing the heat from his head to escape through its weaved palms.

Unlike his hat, one piece of gear that Mike had retained was a set of gloves, which he had put on earlier that morning in preparation for rowing. He had bought them on a whim at Walmart the day before the race and, while he didn't know exactly what sport they were designed for, he suspected they would come in handy during the adventure. They were black leather on the inside, a woven blend of cotton and nylon on the outside of the hand, and they stopped at the second knuckle. Mike had cut off the Velcro retaining strap thinking it would chafe if he did any serious rowing. He would offer them to John when his turn for rowing came up, but was not sure his brother would use them. Mike was embarrassed at the softness of his hands, the manifestation of a profession where typing reports was typically the most physical use of his hands during the course of a day. John's hands were rougher and calloused, hands that had regularly been used in fighting for survival.

It was a long row. Venice Canal was as flat as melted

butter, like the pool water that insects could walk on without breaking through. And it was quiet, the morning light shimmering in a silence broken only by the sounds of Mike's oars cutting through the water and pushing the boat forward, six feet at a time. The rhythm of the oar strokes reverberated gently off the canal's steep retaining walls, and John quickly fell asleep in the front of the boat to the lullaby of his brother's toils.

Not a significant word had been said since they folded up the maps and launched the boat into the canal. Mike looked over his shoulder at his brother and thought of the verbal sparring of the night before. Assuredly John suffered from PTSD, and as he watched him curled up asleep in the front of the boat, Mike could not help but wonder what terrible and unspoken events his brother had lived through. It came so easy to handle issues in jest, and maybe there was some second purpose hidden in their taunts that helped them both to cope with the issues, but Mike had vowed to find a moment during the trip to tell his brother how proud he was of John's service to the country, how grateful he was for the sacrifices John and his military brothers had endured on behalf of those who remained safely back home. But while the thoughts came easy as he stroked through the water and glanced upon his older brother sleeping, the words would not be spoken now, but he vowed again he would find the strength to say them aloud before the trip was over.

It was a long row. The sun was fully awake and the sweat ran down Mike's face underneath the cheap tourist hat as he stroked the oars, pushing the boat slowly down the canal. He rested for a minute as he took an old bandana and tied it around his head underneath the hat to stop the sweat from dripping into his eyes. He had pulled out one of the gallon bottles of water and told himself to rest the oars and drink every hundred strokes. He did not bother to count the strokes nor look at his watch. There was rowing to do, and neither the number of strokes taken nor the time elapsed seemed to have much significance. He wondered what had been the most difficult aspect of war for his brother. He guessed that if any of John's men had been killed while under his supervision it would be the greatest pain of all. Mike had long been in law enforcement, and while he had handled a few fatal traffic accidents, and had pointed his weapon in the line of duty, he had never seen anyone actually die, and had never been involved in any form of shooting incident.

His brother had always been a natural leader, the type of man other men want to follow during difficult times. He seemed to exude increased calmness the worse situations became, but at the same time, was able to effectively assess the situation and come up with the best course of action before anyone else even realized what was going on. He never yelled or panicked, his instructions delivered so effortlessly that their significance was sometimes lost on those who didn't know him well.

When they were still in high school, there were regular summer family reunions at beach locations typically in northeast Florida. Distant family relatives would come together and put the "fun" in a dysfunctional family. Bonfires would be lit on the beach and great quantities of beer consumed, as stories grew louder and laughter and challenges filled the air. Mike could still remember the time when, with the sun going down and the air filled with talk and laughter, John had quickly stood up and coolly instructed Mike to call 9-1-1, their cousin was caught in a rip current. Without another word, John ran to the surf and swam the 100 yards to his ten-year-old cousin, pulling him out of the current and back to the beach coughing up foam. Mike had raced to the house to call 9-1-1 as instructed, and it was only as he went racing back to the beach to help his brother that anyone else in the family realized what was going on. Of course, John was the hero of the party later that night, but it was the fact that he had seen what others hadn't, known immediately what to do, and did it without hesitation that made him different than other men. It was often hard to discern this quality in men, especially if they were snoring in the bow of a small boat, but Mike knew what his brother was made of, and respected him more than any other man he knew.

It was a long row, but finally the man-made Venice Canal opened up to the northern end of Lemon Bay. While the bay would slowly grow in width, it was still too narrow to allow enough wind for the sails, so Mike rested for a minute, drank some more water, and then resumed his rowing.

John had seemed naturally bound for the military since

as far back as Mike could remember, although there didn't ever seem to be a defining moment or influencing incident; it just seemed where he was intended to be. There weren't any close relatives in the military and, when John had joined, it was not a very popular place to make a career. But it didn't seem like he ever had any doubt. On a regular basis in high school, and then in college, he discussed his entry into the army as if it was already a done deal.

He had applied to the military academies, but the family lacked the political connections and there was nothing that could be put on paper to make John stand out from the many other qualified candidates. He had received a significant scholarship offer from a prestigious military school in South Carolina, but it would still cost much more than he could afford, and the combined scholarship and in-state tuition offered by the University of Florida proved irresistible. He studied engineering and was one of the few native-born males in most of his classes, which were typically dominated by foreign students who were much more serious about their educations than most American kids. He loved his studies, did well, and struck a fair balance between schoolwork and his extracurricular pursuits, which, of course, included ROTC.

While John had been interested in becoming a Navy SEAL, he had pursued the Army upon graduation, as the opportunities to get involved in Special Operations seemed greater. He successfully pursued and completed Ranger training at the first opportunity and, while he never talked about it, there were additional periods of unspecified training that Mike assumed must have been related to additional Special Ops work associated with his ranger duties.

Like many soldiers, John didn't like to talk about his work and, although Mike had no point of comparison, he hoped it was just a matter of not talking about the topics with those outside of the Service, those who couldn't understand the dynamics of the situation. Mike prayed his brother had talked more about his job to his military brethren, because he had sure been mute on the issue with his own blood brother.

John had seemed headed down the road to Special Ops work when the wars in Iraq and Afghanistan broke out, and he had apparently switched over to conventional duty. He had occasionally made a passing comment that there wasn't anything all that special in special operations, and it was better to have the clarity and predictability of conventional warfare when you were responsible for other men's lives.

Whatever his assignments and commands, and John spoke rarely about either, he had apparently done well and earned the rank of Lt. Colonel shortly before returning home for rest and relaxation in the form of a little boating adventure with his wayward younger brother. Despite the lack of communication, Mike did regularly think and worry about his brother, and was happy when he saw the change in rank inconspicuously noted on an email asking for assistance for an injured soldier relocating to Tampa.

Mike had thought that the heightened rank must surely have moved his brother further from the hostile front—it certainly worked that way in police work.

As the breadth of Lemon Bay gradually expanded, Mike could feel the breeze start to pick up. Soon, the chop of waves would similarly increase and, before he raised the sails, Mike knew it would be a good time to release some of the water he had been so conscientiously drinking. The "bucket" was something John had taught him about long ago, lecturing on the number of solo sailors who lost their lives in the apparently simple act of evacuating their bladders or bowels. Appearances can be deceiving John had warned, and even the simplest acts can have disastrous consequences when you were in a small boat on a big bay in a bigger world. The trick, John had said, was to think in advance about how you would feel seeing the boat sail away by itself with you stuck in the dark cold water trying to remember the prayers they had taught you in grade school. Was it worth the convenience of hanging your ass or pecker over the side of the boat?

And so Mike pulled the bucket from under the center plank and placed it immediately in front of his knees on the centerline of the boat. With his wet suit uncomfortably zipped down as low as it would go, he waited for his stream to begin.

"What the hell…" John said groggily as he turned over from his slumber in the front of the boat. "I thought I was dreaming that I was a firefighter and someone had opened up the valve for the hose."

"You're just jealous because you can still remember when you could piss like this. In a few more years, even the memories will pass," Mike responded with a chuckle as he started to worry that he was going to overfill the bucket, an event that he definitely had not thought of in advance.

After dumping the contents overboard and rinsing the bucket out, Mike began letting the sails out. "Damn, that was a sweet sleep," John said. "Can't remember the last time I got that deep; how long has it been?" Mike smiled but gave no indication it had been almost 4 hours, not the single hour they had agreed upon. While he said nothing, he was overwhelmed with contentment that his brother had slept, and slept well, while he was at the oars.

With no answer to his question, John looked at his watch and grunted with disgust. "Yo, let me take my turn," he said as he moved to the back of the boat and tried to assert himself in rigging the small sail.

"Sit back down old man," Mike said as he rebuffed the approach. "I've got the helm, and all is well. Enjoy the view as this master sailor shows you how it's done."

"It is a helluva view," John agreed as he looked around the empty bay, enjoying the soft breeze that was kicking up, watching the birds work along the mangroves.

"Did you have sweet dreams during your nap?" Mike asked. "I've often wondered what dogs and old men dream about when they're sleeping. Were you chasing some rabbits, or maybe you go back to days of youth, when you were strong and bold?"

"I don't remember, but pretty sure I wasn't chasing any rabbits … and I'm not sure there was ever a time when I was strong and bold. Well, maybe … before the Army beat it out of me."

"Speaking of which," Mike responded, "are you getting laid? I mean, anything regular? I guess I should ask first if you're still able to even do it—maybe I should first ask if you remember what sex is?"

"Right out of the box with you. Every day. Right from the get-go. Is there anything you think about other than sex, drinking, and arresting bad guys? I don't even want to think about the content of your dreams. Do your thoughts ever rise above the basest instincts? Are you able to communicate, even briefly, in a fashion that doesn't immediately reveal your complete self-absorption and preoccupation with the lowest forms of self-entertainment?"

"Okay," Mike said, "let me rephrase it: Brother, I was wondering if, since last we met, you have become engaged in any serious relationships—perhaps a companion who has brought you joy and contentment?"

"That was better. But alas, the answer is no. It is a sad state of affairs; the Army has yet to issue me a girlfriend, let alone a wife. I was thinking about that on the flight home. I have to admit, it is a pretty poor situation. There have been a couple of occasions where I think there was a spark, but it was always with uniformed subordinates, and there is nothing good that comes of that. I know you'll find this hard to believe, but the last time I was with a girl was over a year ago. You just get focused on other things over there; it doesn't seem to cross your mind as much. And you're always so damn tired whenever you get some down time, all you want to do is sleep."

"Tell me about the year ago if that's the best you have," Mike said.

"It was nothing. We were on R&R in Germany. We met at a party, and she just seemed … I don't know … comfortable. Didn't ask a lot of questions, was smart and confident. Maybe she just felt sorry for me," John said as he thought back.

"What was her name?"

"Allison. I was supposed to stay with her for a couple of nights a few months ago when I was transiting Germany on a TDY, but she had to go to some conference. She's a teacher at a university in Germany. I was thinking I should call her and visit on the way home for this trip, but I didn't want to be late for this big adventure. I could be lying in her soft bed right now instead of this hard plywood.

"You gonna let me take the rudder or not?" John asked, changing the topic to something he was more ready to discuss.

"Nope," Mike said, "but you can tug that main halyard a little bit; looks like I didn't get the sail all the way up. If the wind is good, I think we'll make Don Pedro Park in a couple of hours."

The wind did abide and the small boat moved along, seeming to share the boys' contentment as she performed the duties for which she was built. It was not a fast pace; you could run faster over a short distance, but she was diligent and persistent. With a squared bow, she was not pretty to the eye, and she did not so much cut through waves as she shouldered through them. But she was a tough little boat, stable at the beam and sturdy as a goat. With a regular breeze she produced a low thumping beat that was a perfect cadence to the whispering air pushing her along, a rocking lullaby that instilled confidence in a sailor. It was not the type of beauty that bedazzled the eye; it was something that took time and experience to appreciate. The boat knew what she was built for, she was confident in her purpose, and she loved to be sailed. There was something rare and pure about the little boat, pushing through waves without question or hesitation, always ready and true to her calling.

As the boat balanced with the wind, Mike reached under the plank and drew out his last bottle of booze. He twisted open the cap, and it dawned on him that there might not be a liquor store in his immediate future, but he swallowed the thought, along with the bourbon, reminding himself that the future was a figment, a lying and manipulative witch to which he had promised he would give no more. He held the bottle quietly as he enjoyed the view, appreciating the absence of motorboats and the damn jet skis, feeling drenched in the sunshine and the peaceful rocking harmony of the sea, the wind, and the boat. He wished John would share some of the bourbon, but then mocked himself as he remembered the cliché about misery loving company.

By mid-afternoon they had reached Don Pedro State Park on Little Gasparilla Island at the southern end of Lemon Bay. The barrier island was approximately eight miles long and, as there were no bridges from the mainland, it was obviously less congested than the several huge golf courses that sat immediately to its east. The park was a relatively isolated rock outcropping on the northeast side of the island, and the race checkpoint was located in the middle of this outcropping.

This northern part of the island, including the check-in point, was protected in double depth, the first layer consisting of a shallow ring of sharp coral, with an inner layer comprised of a seemingly impenetrable lacework of mangrove trees. There was a small point on the southeast side of the outcropping however, where the coral had been ground into sand, and the grasp of the mangroves had loosened enough to allow visitors to establish a small path to the park. Mike sailed parallel to the mangroves and, when he saw the spot, turned the boat into the wind, which was coming in over the island. They floated gently toward the point where the path started and tied the boat up to one of the mangrove trees. They listened as the unique kaleidoscope of noise that came from the mangrove swamps briefly stopped, the inhabitants allowing the visitors to introduce themselves, and then resumed when the boys appeared to have nothing threatening to say.

"It's too hot to wear these f'ing dry suits anymore,"

Mike said, as he waded up to the path and then began to strip the gear off from the lower half of his body.

"Amen," John said, following the same course of action. "I was thinking that if you could also install a fan in the front of the boat it would help my napping experience."

"Didn't look to me like you needed any help in the napping department there Ol' Man Wriggley," Mike retorted, as he came back to the boat and put the dry suit under the plank in the front of the boat while also pulling his beach booties out of the same gear bag. At the same time, he opened the bottle back up and took a few mouthfuls as he looked around and said, "It's pretty now, but in two months, this place will be so thick with mosquitoes they'd be eating your eyeballs."

The boys headed up the path for about 100 yards before it opened up into a small sandy patch of about 25 square yards crowded with gnarly old pine trees that had seen their share of hurricanes. This is where the first check-in point had been and, while there was no one there to greet them now, there was a quiet sense of satisfaction in having actually made it that far.

"What the hell are you doing?" John asked as Mike hummed some barely audible tune and danced with his arms folded on his chest, picking up one leg after the other, bent at the knee, listing to port and starboard, as he slowly moved in a circle.

"It isn't obvious? I'm dancing a jig. I wasn't sure we would make it this far, and it is an accomplishment worthy of celebration. Think of our mother, up in Heaven, smiling down on this beautiful day, watching her two boys play nice together and doing manly things. Damn, I wish we'd done this sooner."

Without saying a word, John linked his arm through Mike's, recognizing the tune as an old Irish ditty their father used to sing, and joined in the jig. Time is a hard thing to comprehend if you ever give it any significant thought, and somehow, the boys' little jig spanned thirty years of victories and regrets, love and losses, time spent well, and some just pissed away.

"That was fun. Thanks," John said as the jig came to an end.

"I'd toast your seamanship, but the bottle is down at the boat, and besides, it's my last bottle and I don't want to waste it on someone as sober as you," Mike replied.

Instead, Mike pulled out the navigational charts and laid them on the sandy ground. The next leg of the trip would start with approximately ten nautical miles through a narrowing stretch of the Intercoastal that paralleled Little Gasparilla Island before opening back up into Placida Harbor and then Gasparilla Sound. There would then be a significant stretch of deeper open water as they crossed the mouth of Port Charlotte before returning to the shallower water of Pine Island Sound.

Staring silently at the map, both brothers focused on the crossing of Port Charlotte. In terms of size, the harbor was inconsequential, only eight kilometers wide at its broadest points. What concerned the boys was that the narrow mouth of the harbor, an approximate one kilometer, cut through the barrier islands of Gasparilla on the north and Cayo Costa on the south. The depth of the water in this channel grew quickly to thirty-five feet as, four times a day, half the liquid contents of the entire port swept through the cut in racing fulfillment of lunar obligations. In the process, anything close to the vortex of this fast-moving stream generally went the way of the tide, and there was no wind strong enough to allow the little boat to resist the force of this tidal pull. Further complicating matters was the fact that the harbor had significant commercial maritime business, big boats that would be navigating the same cut with no room to make allowances for a little sailboat bobbing on the waves like a leaf in the breeze. It was no Tampa Bay, but it brought back bad memories. And in the far back of their minds was the knowledge that every significant predator in the sea considered the outgoing tides to be a loudly ringing dinner bell, providing a smorgasbord of delights swept along the currents into the Gulf of Mexico.

"It's getting late, but if I've been reading the water right, I think we should hit the gap pretty close to slack tide," John said. Then, giving voice to what they were both thinking, he added, "But it always seems to come back to timing, and after our debacle in Tampa, I sure don't like the thought of being anywhere near that cut in darkness."

"Oh, the naysaying and nail-biting … there is no worthwhile reward without risk. Think of it as an opportunity for redemption. An opportunity to correct the course of events, to make our mark with intent rather than by happenstance, to stand and prove ourselves worthy of life's challenges," Mike said.

"Oh boy, here we go again," was all that John could say in response.

VIII

There was something about trying to survive in a small boat that lessened your need to go to the bathroom, but both men took the opportunity to evacuate their bladders and bowels on firm ground before returning to the boat. They walked back down to discover that a raiding party of two raccoons had boarded the boat. When Mike saw one trying to open the bottle of bourbon, he charged with rage, waving his arms and shouting, "Let go of my hooch you little bastard." But the raccoon, not impressed, stood up on two legs, extended his own arms, and hissed back in preparation for making a launch at Mike. The unexpected resistance not only silenced Mike's shouts of rage, it scared the crap out of him. While he tried to make a hard right to buy some time and avoid an immediate physical confrontation with the raccoon, his booze-soaked brain told his knees to simply buckle, causing him to fall ungracefully into the shallow water and coral rock on his right side. Humiliated but not defeated, he summoned back his manhood and stood up, eying the hissing raccoon carefully.

"All right, you little fucker, you're tough, I'll give you that. But that is my whiskey, and it's my last bottle, and I'm more than happy to fight to the death right here and now." He approached the raccoon slowly, deliberately, but without any specific plan of action. He was no longer shouting in rage, but the raccoon quickly sensed that the quietly approaching human had more than a few loose screws and was much more dangerous than the ones who shouted and jumped around. With a head nod to his buddy, the two quickly scampered out of the boat and into the mangroves, empty-handed.

"Never, never ever, is there a dull moment with you, my brother," John said.

"I can't believe that little bastard was going after my booze. Take the fucking granola bars … or the MREs. Hell, I'll even heat them up for you. But no, he had to go for the one thing I give a shit about. Come on out here and settle this like a man, you little pussy!" Mike yelled as he searched the mangroves. "Well, to the victor belong the spoils," he announced as he opened the bottle and took a large mouthful, swishing it around in his mouth before tilting his head back and letting it slowly trickle down his throat.

The afternoon was getting late as they untied the boat from the mangroves and headed south. John had once again sought the helm, but Mike asserted his privilege as master-planner and had taken the rudder in one hand and the bottle of Wild Turkey in the other. There was a strong breeze, and the dark clouds building over the mainland revealed thunderstorms that were unlikely to make it to the Intercoastal. In three hours, they had made it past Placida Harbor and into Gasparilla Sound.

The sandy beaches at the southern end of Gasparilla Island were on their right as they began to enter Charlotte Harbor and, with the sun close to the horizon, John could not help but comment hopefully, "Damn, those beaches sure look like they'd be a lot more comfortable place to camp for the evening than this little boat." Mike said nothing as he worked his way past the halfway mark of his bottle.

The wind and the waves picked up as the boat slowly worked its way into the bay. Inevitably, the thunderstorm to the east, the one that should have stayed over the mainland, drew closer, and a soft rain began to fall, limiting visibility in the waning light. But Mike remained silent, his humor giving way to a darkness that seemed to match the approaching thunderstorm. Reflecting back on the capsizing in Tampa Bay, and his thought at the time that he wished he had drunk a lot less or a lot more, he chose the latter, and worked at the bottle with the same blind determination that was apparent in his drive to move the boat forward in spite of the circumstances.

The sun was setting just to the north of Gasparilla as they reached the cut between the two barrier islands. The channel was still discernible, however, marked by a change in color associated with the deeper water. They had missed slack tide and the water was beginning to increase its tempo as it funneled the bay's contents out and into the Gulf. The storm moved closer, providing needed propulsion for the boat, but increasing the height of waves to the point that Mike could not see the channel markers when he was in the troughs. Other than having a large commercial fishing boat bearing down on them, there seemed little else that could possibly go wrong.

He sat drunkenly at the rudder, smiling and softly humming a tune while forcing the boat forward. He seemed able to comprehend the dire nature of the situation, and it wasn't that he didn't care; he seemed to be enjoying the unfolding events. He pushed the little boat beyond her limits and smiled as the rain struck so hard he thought it might have turned to hail, pulling as much as he could from the bottle before its miserable end.

A third of the way through the channel, the boat began to slam up and down in the waves hard enough that gear began to break free, jumping into the sea rather than staying in the boat with a maniac at the helm. The darkness of the storm and night melted into the colors of the water, the border imperceptible to mortal vision. He willed the boat forward into waves he could not see, silently hoping for that violent pinnacle that would send the boat into splinters and provide him relief from his grief. Drunkenly humming the old ditty of his youth, he commanded her forward, dizzily feeling the world spin at full velocity, confident that he was finally about to find deliverance.

But it was not to be. As the rushing tide diffused out into the Gulf of Mexico, pushing the sturdy little boat along for the ride, the fury of the waves subsided, and the storm surrendered to the cool waters. Mike tilted his head back and noticed the rain had stopped and a canopy of stars hung over the boat. Feeling his eyes start to close, his back and stomach loosened, and his butt slid toward the center of the boat, his torso slumping against the side of the boat as his hand fell away from the tiller.

"Did you hear that?" John asked.

In his drunken stupor, Mike could barely lift his eyelids. But his brother had asked a question, and he felt compelled to answer for as long as he was conscious. "Hear wha … you say?" he responded as best he could.

"It sounds like a girl," John continued as he looked around the boat.

"A girl … wha' da fuck? No … I don't … no shit … no girl."

"Shut up and listen you drunken asshole. I heard a girl yelling."

Mike did not respond. But neither did he pass out. He burped and he listened, disgusted with his consciousness. And then he heard it. Or at least, he thought he heard. It sounded like a woman yelling "help." But it couldn't be; they were out in the Gulf of fucking Mexico in the dark of night. There was no chick yelling for help; it was just the booze.

"Help me!" Mike heard it again.

Amused, he yelled back, without lifting his head up, "I

can't … I'm too fuckin' drunk."

"Nice," John said. "Get your ass up and find her shithead."

"I jus' fucking tol' you … I can't; you fucking save her," John slurred. "I haf' go nighty-night now."

John kicked him hard in the thigh, prompting a howl from Mike. "Jackass, this ain't about you right now. Do the right thing."

Mike dragged himself back into sitting position and looked into the blackness around him.

"Hey, anyone out dere?" was all he was able to manage.

"Over here," a female voice responded. The sound was clear enough that Mike turned his head around and felt a tinge of sobriety. *You gotta fuckin' be kidding me,* he thought in his dizzying drunken stupor. *This can't be happening.*

As he looked behind the boat, he saw what appeared to be someone swimming after the boat, which was now again moving south under its own command. He pushed the tiller hard away, and the boat came about and then sat still with the sails luffing in the wind.

He watched listlessly as the figure swam toward the boat, and finally, a hand appeared on the toe rail. A second hand quickly followed, and then an elbow. Mike tried to hold his head up to watch the events. The boat tilted hard to one side as the figure threw a leg over the rail and then hoisted itself into the boat. He watched numbly as the small figure came to rest mostly on the bottom of the boat but also draped over the center plank. With his head still hanging down loosely, he made out two bare legs sticking out of a pair of cutoffs. It was a woman, and she wore nothing but the shorts. He made eye contact with her but said nothing.

The woman looked at him hard and long, saying nothing, but assessing the situation. Mike's head fell back down, and his eyes closed.

The woman was kicking him and talking. He tried to pick his head back up.

"Was there somebody else with you? I heard you talking to someone," she asked.

Mike looked in her eyes and shook his head no, mumbling, "Just me."

He took in a big breath, slowly and with great effort, as if every one of his ribs were broken, and then let it out in a heavy sigh. With all his strength, he forced himself to ask, "You sail?" She nodded yes in response. He raised a heavy hand, wobbly pointing east toward Cayo Costa, and said, "That way." Then he fell on his side and slid into the numb blackness of unconsciousness.

IX

Lieutenant Colonel John Rudyard Kelly was buried at Arlington National Cemetery on the morning of October 18th, approximately six months before he would have returned home and gone on a small sailboat endurance challenge with his younger brother, Michael.

Mike had received the news at work. Upon returning to his office in the afternoon, he was advised he had visitors, and when he saw the formal and somber-looking military uniforms, he immediately started to feel dizzy; he had never contemplated how such a situation might unfold, never contemplated that his brother would precede him. After suggesting the need for privacy, they had gone into one of the interrogation rooms and relayed the profound condolences of the Secretary of the Army. His knees shook for the first time in his life, and he was unable to speak. They provided reference materials and paperwork, but it was almost as if he had gone deaf.

They left, and then he left. Picked up a bottle on the

way home and drank until he passed out.

The funeral at Arlington had been one of a dozen that day, each the saddest and most mournful day in the lives of the survivors standing around the multiple holes in the ground. Mike remembered that he had completed forms regarding the ceremony, but could not remember anything about them, including when or how he had filled them out. It all worked out in the end.

There was a full Catholic Mass in the Chapel at Fort Myers. He had declined the offer of a military escort band for the funeral procession, although he had gone along with someone's suggestion for a drummer. From the chapel, they walked to the gravesite, his brother's body placed on a caisson pulled by six large white horses, the drummer marking time the entire way. John had posthumously been given some type of medal and promoted to colonel as a result of events associated with his death. The increased rank meant his caisson was accompanied by a riderless horse, sword hanging from the saddle and boots placed backwards in the stirrups to signify that the rider had fallen. It struck Mike as appropriate.

There had been a bugler at the graveside, and his call of retreat had been the most woeful sound Mike ever heard. Tears ran down his face the entire time, but they flowed like rain when they approached him with the flag from John's coffin. *Surely,* he thought, *there must be someone else in this big world to whom they can hand that flag. Someone more deserving ... someone who can make sense of it all;*

someone who had earned the sacrifice. But the bearer gave the flag to Mike, the only living relative at the funeral.

The report of the rifles closed the proceedings. Several of John's military brothers had tried to convey messages of respect and admiration, but it was lost on Mike. The body of John Kelly was put into the hole to be covered with dirt.

X

The sun was coming up bright, but Mike Kelly was still damp from the prior evening. He lay in the bottom of his brother's boat, his lower half still in the shade. While his view was limited by his position in the boat, he could hear the waves coming onto shore nearby, and the stability of the boat let him know that he was on dry land somewhere.

The woman sat on the front plank of the boat looking at him warily. She held one of his gallon jugs of water and was eating one of his granola bars. He remembered the cutoff jeans from the night before, but she was now wearing one of his shirts. She said nothing as they looked at each other. She was in her late 20s, maybe early 30s, and looked to be five foot five. She had short blonde hair and wore no shoes. She wasn't heavy, but it was impossible to discern her figure under the billowing shirt she had poached from his gear bag. He guessed she was strong; she was apparently a pretty good swimmer.

He turned to his side and rested for a second before

starting to push himself up. He sat on the aft plank of the boat with his back turned toward the woman, and looked around. The boat had been pulled up on a sand beach and he could see what he thought was the Gasparilla Cut several hundred yards to the north. There was no one else around and, under other circumstances, it would have been the start of a beautiful day. A pod of porpoises was feeding just off the beach to their north.

He rose slowly from the plank, letting his back unfold as he carefully stretched out his arms and stepped out on the port side of the boat. He walked around the back of the boat, noting that the rudder had been properly lifted from its mount before hitting ground, thus avoiding damage. He looked north again at what he presumed was the cut he had sailed through the prior evening, and then south at a long strip of apparently uninhabited beach. He bent over and then squatted, watching the fins of the porpoises rise as they took in air and then submerged to resume their fishing. He walked out to the beach and pissed into the waves.

He came back to the boat along the starboard side, amazed at the lack of any serious damage. The little boat was apparently indestructible. Coming around the bow and completing his circle, he looked at the water jug and stuck out his hand toward the woman. She handed him the jug. There was still a fifth of the contents left and he drank it all, throwing the empty plastic container into the front of the boat.

He looked again at the woman, and she looked at him,

neither saying anything. She had a heavy bruise below her left eye and maybe some bruising around her neck. The outer part of her right thigh was bruised for almost the entire length, marked with the deep blue color that indicated significant trauma.

He nodded his head for her to get out of the boat, and she obliged. He started to pull the boat back down to the sea.

"Can you bring me over to the mainland?" she asked.

Without looking at her he nodded his head to the east and said, "It's over that way. You're a good swimmer. Or you can wait here and wave someone down; it won't be long till some powerboater comes by."

"Come on, chief, that's gotta be a three-mile swim. I had a kinda hard night too … how 'bout cutting me some slack?"

He looked at her and looked north and south again. Nodding to the cut he had sailed through the prior evening, he said, "That way is backwards for me. I'm in a race and headed south. If we're where I think we are, Sanibel Island is about ten to twelve miles south. I'm going on the outside of the island, and it will probably be a little rough. If you want, I'll put you out there."

She helped him push the boat out into the surf. He took up the oars and rowed several hundred yards out beyond the break before putting up the sail and heading south.

It was a good day for sailing. There was a stiff breeze from the west, and while the waves were bigger than those of the ICW, they were smoother and rolling in nature as compared with the chop of the shallower water. The water was saltier but free of the mangrove refuse and motorboat discharge. The color wasn't the bluish-black of real ocean waters, but it was a deep green with a head of foam that let you know it was big and wild enough to do whatever it wanted. The boat seemed to relish its continued life, loving the change of pace, rolling up and down on the waves as the water went rushing by, sails tight and humming in the breeze.

"Thanks for picking me up last night," the woman said thirty minutes after leaving the beach. Mike nodded his head in acknowledgment but kept his focus on where the boat was headed. He hadn't really picked her up the prior evening, although he did have a vague recollection of trying to stop the boat and help. Way down deep inside, he was embarrassed by being drunk in front of other people, especially strangers. But he certainly hadn't entertained the possibility of any company the prior evening and, well, basically he just didn't give a shit anymore.

"Something big bumped my leg right before I saw you. Pretty sure I was about to be fish chow."

He looked at her to see if she was bullshitting; she wasn't. He looked her in the eye for the first time, and she looked directly back. Her eyes were not fearful, neither were they needful, nor wanting, nor misty, dreaming, tearful, or brooding. They were the eyes of life: focused, alert, responsive. They were the color of well-treated, but weathered, mahogany wood. Grains of a deep brown that was connected to everything on land, with a quality that exuded warmth and perceptiveness. Her teeth were white and, despite the swelling bruise, any smile that crossed her face would be genuine and powerful.

The trip passed without incident or further conversation and, three hours later, he headed into a small marina in what he guessed was the town of Sanibel. They pulled up at a small bait store and the woman tied the boat up to a dock post.

Mike threw the empty plastic milk jugs onto the dock, pulled his small personals bag out of the box under the center plank, and then hoisted himself out of the boat. He picked up the jugs and went to find a source of fresh water. When he got back the woman was gone, and he tossed the filled jugs into the boat. He entered the bait store and walked its full three aisles, putting some smoked fish wrapped up in tin foil and some more granola bars into a basket.

"Where's the nearest liquor store?" he asked the clerk as he was paying for his purchase.

"No hablo," the man responded without looking at Mike.

"Donde es el tienda de whiskey mas proxima?" Mike attempted wearily.

"No intiendo," the man said, again without looking up.

"Listen motherfucker," Mike said, his voice quickly rising, "you intiendo me just fine. I ain't in any mood to put up with your shit. Look at me, and tell me where the closest liquor store is, or I might just do something you'll regret."

The man finally looked up, but somehow, he now had a gun in his hand as he said, "No, you are the fuckermother."

The woman seemed to come from nowhere and inserted herself between the two, pushing Mike with her back toward the door. Once Mike was out the door, she returned to the clerk. "Lo siento mucho, por favor perdónanos. Mi hermano tiene una enfermedad psicológica. Pero puede usted por favor decirme donde está la tienda de liqour cercana es?" The clerk smiled at her fluency and advised the liquor store was two blocks down the street.

The woman came out and found Mike sitting with his legs hanging off the dock next to the boat. She sat beside him and told him where the liquor store was. He nodded his head in appreciation.

"Sorry about that, I just...." He didn't finish the sentence, and she didn't respond.

"Wouldn't have figured you for a Spanish speaker," he said. The woman just shrugged her shoulders. Mike wasn't used to being on the talking side of a one-way conversation.

"You got someone coming to pick you up?" he asked.

The woman appeared to be thinking as she looked out at the Gulf. But it didn't seem like she was thinking about the answer to the question, more like she was deciding if she was going to talk to him at all.

"No," she finally said, looking at him directly. "I'm living up in Pensacola. I've gotta find a way to get up there pretty quickly. I've got something important to take care of."

Mike instinctively went into active-listening mode. It was a skill that had served him well during his years in law enforcement. Most people talked a lot of shit, but there were some people, you had to really pay attention to what they were saying. They used their words carefully, and if you paid attention, they answered your questions and a lot more.

"I guess you weren't just out for an evening swim last night, huh?" he said, realizing that she obviously had no money or other means of support in the pockets of the tight cutoff jeans. Momentarily escaping the confines of his own world, he wondered about the circumstances that led to her being swept out into the Gulf of Mexico.

She found amusement in the comment and smiled for the first time. "No," she said. "It was practice. I'm going to attempt to backstroke all the way to Mexico next month." Mike smiled.

"You said you were in a race ... that EcoLoco thing?"

"Yeah," Mike answered.

"Bad news, chief, you ain't gonna make it by the deadline in that boat."

"It's not like that ..." Mike responded. "it's a challenge, not a race."

"Yeah, well, we both know the race ain't your challenge

either, Detective."

Mike was impressed, and that didn't happen very often anymore. How the hell had she figured out he was a cop? he wondered. The comment put him on the defensive, and he tried to switch the conversation back to her.

"So you got a deadline of your own; you said you needed to get back to Pensacola quickly. What's your race?"

"You don't want to know," she said as she looked back at the Gulf.

Mike stood up and took out his wallet. "The pin code is 2042 if you need to get some cash from an ATM," he said as he handed her a credit card. She looked at the credit card and then at him, but didn't reach out to take it.

"You can pay me back when you get your stuff squared away," he said with his outstretched hand still offering the card. She was looking and thinking, but she wasn't saying anything, and she sure wasn't reaching to accept the card.

Putting the credit card back into the wallet, he gently tossed the wallet toward her, and she reflexively caught it. "Take the whole thing; it ain't doing me any good."

She looked at him and said nothing. She took out the credit card and tossed the wallet back to him. "I'm probably gonna be charging about seven grand over the next few days. I'll pay you back in three weeks." Mike just shrugged his shoulders and started to get into the boat.

She looked at the credit card and asked, "What department are you with, Mike Kelly?"

"Hillsborough," he responded, starting to untie the line

to the boat.

"Aren't you forgetting your supplies at the liquor store?" she asked.

"I changed my mind," he said as he pushed away from the dock and broke out the oars.

"My name is Erin," she said as he started to row away.

"Good luck, Erin. I hope it works out for you."

"See you in few days," she said. Her words were deliberate, and he wondered what she meant. But he said nothing as he rowed out of the marina.

XI

Sanibel effectively marked the southern end of the Intercoastal Waterway. There were still forty miles of crowded Gulf coastline between Sanibel and Marco Island, the point at which mankind had, thus far, given up on its battle to subdue the wild expanse known as the Everglades. The 100 miles south of Marco Island were marked by a different kind of battle, as the freshwater Everglades mixed it up on a daily basis with the salty Gulf of Mexico. A brown, brackish wilderness with so many threats that focusing on any one in particular almost certainly doomed you to another.

Most recently, the Burmese python had moved to top billing among the denizens of this area. There were many stories about how these snakes had come to invade the everglades, but there was no dispute that, in the twenty years since they arrived, they had risen to a dominant position at the top of the food chain. While the longest python captured in the area had been measured at seventeen feet, there were many sightings, some photographed, of snakes longer than twenty. Amphibious snakes so large they could easily be spotted by airplanes hundreds of feet above. Afraid of nothing, they regularly feasted on deer and wild boar, strangling and suffocating their meals before swallowing them whole. They had been found with the carcasses of alligators, and even crocodiles, in their bellies. It was this silent swimming giant that challengers feared the most when they anchored up at night near the mangroves, alone in this Florida wilderness appropriately known as Ten Thousand Islands.

If you kept your distance from the swamp, however, staying in the greener waters of the Gulf, there was some measure of relief from nightmares of giant snakes sliding over your toe rail. But the python was not the only animal that could eat you in this part of the world. The American Crocodile liked both the green and brown shades of water. The paranoid might think the lack of publicity regarding the thriving crocodile population in this part of Florida was a conspiracy by the tourism industry, but the truth was that the area was so remote, hardly anyone even knew it existed. The average mature male crocodile was fifteen feet long, half again as big as Mike's boat, and weighed in at 800 pounds. Much more aggressive than its better-known cousin the alligator, there were documented reports of it aggressively pursuing small boats and ramming kayakers. While legends of their speed on land were exaggerated, they were easily able to propel themselves in the water up to fifteen mph, three times as fast as any gold medalist human could swim. They could stay out in the ocean for a month and were known to swim hundreds of miles looking for new hunting grounds.

Much more ubiquitous than the crocodiles were bull sharks, which used the Ten Thousand Islands area as a nursery. Uniquely able to adapt to fresh water, the bulls lived their youthful days in the mangroves, feasting on mullet while protected from threats of deeper water. Eventually though, they grew to ten feet in length and were an apex predator all along the coast of Florida, regularly feeding on Blacktip and Lemon sharks. While other sharks, like the Tiger and Great White, had a reputation for taking more human lives, it was thought that many attacks by bulls were improperly classified, as they took place in canals and rivers where most people simply didn't think of ten-foot sharks when considering potential predators.

Of course, there were also giant rays, fifteen feet across, which, when resting on a shallow sand bar and spooked by a small boat, were known to propel themselves in the air, sending occupants akimbo without ever knowing what had hit them. Cottonmouth and Coral snakes might not be as big as the pythons, but a single bite would result in a gruesome, lonely death, far from the nearest hospital or any anti-venom. While black bears and panthers inhabited the Everglades, they typically ceded control of the tidal areas to other predators. With the relentless push of human development from out of Miami, however, their presence could not be ruled out.

While most thought of mosquitoes as irritating pests, they could become so thick in the tidal marshes that large animals died from the blood lost to their bites. There were poisonous plants whose sap had been used to coat arrowheads aimed by Native Americans at invading Spanish conquistadors. In the United States, the Manchineel tree grew only in Florida, and its fruit is known as "the little apple of death." It is one of the most poisonous trees in the world and its toxins are still not fully understood. It oozes droplets of sap from its branches that cause severe blistering upon contact with skin, and even rainwater running off its leaves is toxic.

Of course, there were more immediate, if mundane, threats to survival. The heat of the Florida sun inevitably resulted in dehydration if not properly courted. The wetness and cool evening temperatures of March could easily lead to hypothermia for those whose senses were dulled by the constant demands of survival. A simple slip on a boat deck could crack a skull and, even if it didn't, there was the omnipresent threat of falling overboard and drowning quickly or wasting away as you bobbed around the wetted wilderness. The infamous no-see-ums, or biting midges, were unavoidable even with the best insect repellant, and the red swelling bites left behind paled in comparison with the consequences of the sleep deprivation they induced.

There were, however, still forty miles to go before Mike got to Marco Island, gatekeeper of the Ten Thousand Islands. It was a quiet and sober stretch of sailing. The little boat loved being outside the Intercoastal and plugged along at a steady three knots. The waves were rolling in toward the beach, several hundred yards to the east, and she slid up one side and down the other with the knowing confidence of a skilled craftsman. She loved being salty, and she loved doing her job. She would bring Mike wherever he wanted to go and, while she might not like the heading, it was not her job to set the course. She would go where he wanted, content in performing her duties, determined to keep her master on the proper side of the waterline.

Mike reflected on the developments of recent days. The trip was no longer appealing; he had crashed into potential doom as hard as he could, and somehow he was alive and still sailing south. He thought about giving up on the challenge, beaching the boat and doing something else. But his imagination was impaired, and any land he could conjure up was suffocated by a permanent tropical depression, gray and warm, with feeble threats of a real hurricane.

Besides, he could not help but feel some of the joy the little boat was having as she plied the waves. He thought about the prior evening and his headlong rush into the dark channel in the middle of a thunderstorm. "Thought it was the end … but you handled it all by yourself," he said to the boat.

"*You do not know the day nor the hour,*" the little boat responded gently. Or maybe it was the waves.

Mike nodded in agreement; the boat was right. You

played the cards you were dealt as best you could. He had learned a little bit over the years and, while he knew he would never approach a full understanding, there had been times when he thought he had caught a glimpse into why he was here and what he was supposed to do.

But he was tired and weary, he explained to the boat. Some days his chest felt like an anchor pulling him into a ground made of thick mud. His bones and muscles grew more exhausted with every click of the secondhand, but when he laid down, he could find no sleep, no rest. Surely there must be an end to the misery? he asked. "*Gird your loins,*" whispered the boat, "*be not crushed as if I would leave you.*"

Mike took heed of the encouragement, but observed that the wrong always seemed to outweigh the right; the good faded and the bad thrived. What was the point, he asked, if it doesn't make any difference? "*You don't know what difference it makes,*" the boat responded. "*What is too sublime for you, seek not. Into things that are beyond your strength, search not. Suffering produces endurance, endurance produces character, and character produces hope.*"

Mike pulled out one of the gallon jugs of water and drank thirstily. He opened up the smoked fish and ate it slowly, thinking that it tasted particularly good. He estimated the sun would be setting in an hour, and he headed the boat east toward land. He landed softly on a beach in a wildlife preserve between Naples and Marco Island and set up a small fire and prepared an MRE. He pulled up the center plank of the boat and lay down in his sleeping bag. He pined for some hooch, but couldn't deny a vague sense of betterment for being without it. He slept long and well.

XII

The weather was fair and the wind was firm when Mike woke up the next morning. He had rounded Marco Island by 10:00 am and started sailing southeasterly, trying to stay in the margin that separated Ten Thousand Islands from the Gulf. But the area was a navigational nightmare under the best of circumstances, and Mike was not in the best of circumstances. The expensive GPS system he had bought before the trip had been lost to the bottom of Tampa Bay on the first evening. It wasn't a big deal when all you had to do was keep the mainland on your left and the barrier islands on your right, but, as the name implied, there was no mainland down here, just islands that were really patches of mangroves, and they all looked the same. There were occasional channel markers, but the event sponsors had gone to great lengths to warn that they could not be trusted. Every channel and so-called "island" changed with each passing storm, and there was no passing traffic that was going to come to your rescue if you were in trouble.

The next checkpoint was at Everglades City, a forsaken village buried at the bottom of the everglades whose primary source of income was derived from locals escorting illegal shipments of marijuana and cocaine. The methods were constrained only by imagination; some used airboats to pick up packages dropped by low-flying airplanes, others met mother ships out in the Gulf and then brought the goods in after the end of a genuine fishing trip. It was rumored that there were even small submarines delivering merchandise to the local runners.

Mike would have skipped the checkpoint altogether, but he knew he would be lucky if he still had any water left by the time he got to that point. It would be the only time he planned on penetrating the maze of islands, and the four-mile route through the mangrove islands was as challenging as anything he would do during the trip. First, however, he had to put twenty more miles under his belt to get to the point where he hoped to find the channel that led into the checkpoint.

As soon as he turned to the southeast, the wind died. He took the opportunity to drink as much water as he could and once again unzipped his dry suit as low as it would go. He ate a granola bar, and the crunching sound echoed across the flat milky-brown water. He stopped chewing and listened. *So this is what silence sounds like,* he thought. In all his years, he had never heard such a complete absence of sound. He looked behind him and then slowly in all directions. There was not a single thing moving. No rigging from his boat jangling with the waves or wind, no birds flying, no fish jumping, no waves rolling … not even a ripple. He thought he could actually hear his heart thumping blood through his body just below the sound of his own breathing. *Certainly is different,* he thought as he renewed the cacophony caused by his teeth meeting with the hard granola.

He fastened the sail and then tied the old bandana around his forehead. He put on his gloves and looked at the cheap straw tourist hat he had bought a few days ago, smiling both with amusement and affection. He put the hat on his head and the oars in their locks, and started to row. The air was warm and stale, and the sun was hot, but he rowed all day. He stopped regularly and forced himself to drink as much water as he could hold, and evacuate what he had already consumed into his bucket. At each interval, he took out his charts and tried to figure out where he was. He estimated his speed at two knots, and there didn't appear to be any current other than the constant ebb and flow of the tides into the mangroves. His estimations were little more than guess work, but it made him feel more comfortable, and he was aware it was the most thought he had put into the trip thus far. Aside from these breaks, his mind was clear of thoughts. He rowed, and he looked around at everything and nothing. He tied up to one of the mangrove islands before sunset and, despite the grueling work, felt stronger than when he had started.

He worried about snakes coming from the darkness of

the mangroves, but he could not figure any feasible defense. The MRE he pulled out for the night meal was spaghetti and meatballs and, once again, he savored the taste. While he hated to pollute, he feared the smell of the remnants in the cooking bags might attract unwanted visitors and was tempted to simply toss them into the water for the tide to take away. In the end however, he decided to rinse them out with salt water and stow them under the forward plank. He told himself he had done all he could and laid down in the boat. For the second night in row, he slept well.

He woke on the sixth morning of the challenge to the sound of birds in the mangroves. The sun had broken the horizon, and the sky was quickly changing to the clear light blue of Florida in March. He ate two granola bars and drank as much water as he could hold, looking around with eyes that seemed to see better and a head that seemed less clouded with the clutter of the past and the future.

Once again, there was no wind, and he rowed without complaint. By 1100 hours he estimated he must have rowed past the entry to Indian Key Pass, the channel into Everglades City. He wished he could skip entering into the maze of islands entirely, but he was down to only a quarter gallon of water. He turned the boat around, headed northwest, and rowed for two more hours, looking for the markers that would guide the way to Everglades City. The mangrove islands defied perception. Consisting of the exact same type of foundation and vegetation, it was impossible to tell where one ended and the next started; it was like a mouse trying to see a barn from the other side of a cornfield. Mike hoped the fish at the bottom of Tampa Bay were enjoying knowing where they were with his GPS.

By 1400 hours he was out of water and had not seen anything that looked like a channel marker. Perhaps he had turned around too early the first time. He turned the boat around again, heading back to the southeast, but this time, he moved closer to the islands, hoping to be able to see past the first layer of islands and discern his path. His eyes felt strong, but the flat water meant there was no relief from the reflective light regardless which direction he looked. He began to feel pain from a location he could only describe as behind his eyeballs, a type of pain that he had never felt before. Now, when he most needed to see, the only relief came from closing his eyes.

As he rowed closer, the islands became more distinct, but the many channels between them all looked the same. Some were slightly wider, some seemed to go straight for a little while, but nowhere could he find the channel marker placed by the Army Corp of Engineers. Mike took the charts out for the fourth time that day and studied the shape of the two islands marking the entrance of Indian Key Pass, the head of the channel leading to Everglades City. They were both sufficiently narrow that they might be discernible, and Indian Key itself was marked as an actual land mass rather than a mangrove. It was also one of the few places where the water leading into the maze of islands held a depth of more than ten feet and, even in the waning sun, he might be able to detect the change in the color of the water marking the channel.

Mike continued to row southeast, looking for a land mass that might be Indian Key, or any other type of landmark that would help him figure out how to get to Everglades City. While his eyes alternated looking for a landmark and closing to relieve the pain caused from the sun glare, his mind was assessing the overall situation. He was out of water, the sun was going down, he had made almost no progress during the course of the day, his eyes were failing, and he was not sure where he was. While only a few nights ago, the thought of blasting his way into a watery death had seemed a desirable solution, he did not welcome the thought of withering under the Florida sun, literally rowing himself to death.

Just before sunset, he tied up to one of the mangroves. He was no longer worried about the snakes or crocodiles—he needed water. He prepared an MRE and forced himself to eat half of it before he laid down. He pulled his sleeping bag over his head, hoping for protection from the no-see-ums, and his eyes rejoiced in relief as he closed them in the dark. He went to sleep hoping his plan would bring salvation the following morning.

The sun rose on the seventh morning and woke Mike to the same suffocating stillness he had known since entering the Ten Thousand Islands. The prior afternoon he had suppressed reservations regarding his location and reassured himself that he absolutely had to be somewhere between Fakahatchee Pass and Rabbit Key Pass. He still had his compass and, despite the maze of islands in between, if he could row, or even drag or push his boat four miles northeast, he should be able to enter the more open waters of Chokolosee Bay, which would provide easier navigation to Everglades City and much-needed water.

After untying from the mangroves, he headed southeast and, within an hour, had selected a channel that seemed broad and headed north. He rowed for another hour before the channel turned into a dead end. He rowed halfway back out the channel and took a smaller passage heading northwest. It opened up into a small lagoon and, once again consulting his compass, headed northeast. He picked one of the channels out of the lagoon and rowed until the channel narrowed to the point that he could no longer stroke the oars.

With his beach booties on his feet, he got out of the boat and pulled her through the channel, which eventually opened up to a mud flat. Even without him in the boat, it stuck in the heavy mud, and pulling it forward took all of Mike's reserves. He leaned forward and pulled, the tow rope cutting into his shoulder and his own feet sinking into the mud. One step at a time, always leaning forward, he made it fifty yards over the mud flat to find deeper water.

His right thigh cramped hard as he pulled himself back into the boat, and it was all he could do to straighten the leg and breathe deeply as the boat floated on the flat water.

He was in dire need of fresh water, and as he surveyed his surroundings, he prayed that he had made it into Chokolosee Bay. To the northwest he thought he could see a dock and a boat ramp, and he talked his leg into cooperating as he broke out the oars and started rowing. He rowed with his back to his intended destination, looking over his shoulder to make sure he was on the proper course. But when he finally stopped and turned all the way around, he could no longer see anything that resembled a dock, a boat ramp, or any form of man-made structure.

Mike stood up in the boat to gain a better perspective and immediately felt light-headed. He fought through the dizziness and surveyed the north end of the lagoon. He could see where it appeared to end, and there was nothing to give him any hope that Everglades City was in that direction. Toward the southwest, however, the lagoon seemed to extend beyond his limited field of vision, and he was sure salvation lay in that direction. Within minutes, the muscles in his back, those that had been so reliably pulling the oars, began to cramp into twisted knots, requiring Mike to let go of the oars and cross his arms in front of himself to try to stretch them out.

The sun continued to slowly broil him, but his perspiration grew less and less. He rowed southeast, paralleling the projected shore of Chokolosee Bay, stopping more and more frequently to address the cramping from his back and legs. He stopped looking over his shoulder to see what was coming next, but kept his eyes on the weedy shoreline to his right, hoping to see some sign of civilization.

It was mid-day when Mike detected something different in the environment. He dropped the oars and stretched his back, which was now a single burning knot of cramping pain that no amount of stretching could relieve. He listened but still heard nothing. Then he felt it, a ripple in the glass surface of the lagoon. He cocked his head and could feel it … a breeze. Ever so slight, but still a breeze. He took a heavy breath and begged his back and arms and legs to help him turn around to survey what lay in front of him.

He dared not try to stand up, but lifted one leg and then the other over the plank he was sitting on and looked over the bow of the boat at the direction he was heading. His heart sank as he realized he had rowed to the lagoon's end and, because he had been rowing with the shoreline as his guide, he was now no longer headed southeast. He took out his compass and sighed as it confirmed he had hooked around with the end of the lagoon and was headed southwest. He had searched the entire northeastern shore of the lagoon and there had been no sign of civilization. He was not in Chokolosee Bay; he had no idea where he was.

Refusing to give up, he thought about looking at his charts but realized it would be a waste of time; they could only help you get to where you were going if you already knew where you were. He picked his head up out of his hands and surveyed the western edge of the lagoon, a mangrove forest headed north for as far as he could see. He looked straight ahead again and thought he saw something shining from within the mangroves, shimmering almost. He had been closing his eyes more as he rowed the past several hours and assumed it was a mirage, like the dock and boat ramp he had seen earlier in the day.

There was not enough wind to push the boat, but neither had Mike reached the point of surrender. Without thought, he returned to the rowing position, took up the oars, and pushed the boat toward the shimmering light. An hour later, he reached the western edge of the lagoon and realized that the light had been reflections off waves on the other side of the thin mangrove barrier. There was wind just beyond the mangroves and, as he looked up, he noticed rain clouds in the sky. The thought of fresh water falling from the sky, soothing his burnt skin and blistered hands, falling freely into his open mouth, provided renewed hope and strength.

He looked through the mangrove, a thick web of branches and slippery roots that he estimated was fifty yards deep. He looked to the north and wondered how far it would be till he found a break that would allow him to row or sail the boat back into open water. More than anything, he wanted to be outside of the suffocating confines of the lagoon and the shallow webbed prison it presented. He slowly got out of the boat and into water that was a foot deep. He looked at the boat, and he looked at the mangroves. He asked the boat if his plan was possible, but she wasn't answering.

It was low tide, and he walked into the mangrove, balancing on the slippery roots that were now above water. He pulled on a rope connected to the bow of the boat, but he didn't have the strength to pull her up on the roots with him. He pulled part of the bow up on the roots and tied the rope to a branch, slowly making his way to the back of the boat. He knew his strength was limited and his first push would likely be his best. With every muscle in his body curling up into a ball from lack of water, he knelt down, got his forearms under the boat, and pushed her up onto the roots of the mangrove trees. Once up on the wet roots, she slid forward, and he fell in the same direction, unable to get his arms up in a defensive position as he nose-dived into the roots.

He picked himself up and walked back to the front of the boat, putting the bowline over his shoulder and pulling the boat through the mangrove one careful foot at a time. It was a sense of cold that caused him to realize a soft rain had begun to fall and the water was making its way through the heavy canopy overhead. He rested for a minute, now able to clearly see the open water, the raindrops falling softly on water stirred with a strong breeze. He knew the coldness was not a good sign, that his body might be on the verge of a final shutdown, but the cool water felt so good on his burnt and salty skin.

He pushed onward, carefully balancing himself on the roots and finding a good footing before pulling his loyal boat along the same path. Finally, they reached open water. The boat slid off the mangrove roots, eagerly leading the way. Mike stepped in and pushed the boat away from the mangrove into small but choppy waves. He had no idea of the time of day and considered tying back up to the mangrove while he rested. But he didn't know where he was, and it seemed certain that anyplace the wind and waves took him would be better than where he had just been.

He cut holes in the bottom of the two MRE bags he had stashed under the forward planks and made them into funnels, leading the rainwater into gallon jugs that he securely tied to the oar locks. He pulled his dry suit back up on his torso and zippered it closed. Then he lay down in the boat to rest for a minute. On his back, he opened his mouth and caught the small drops, too tired to swallow but letting them make their own way down his parched throat. His eyes, swollen and closed, wept borrowed tears as the cool moisture puddled in his tear ducts and ran across his eyelids, washing the burning salt away as they slipped down the side of his face. The boat rocked in the waves, happy to be out of the brown water prison. Mike eventually rolled on his side and fell asleep in the rain.

XIII

It was a sound that woke Mike the next day. A sound he had heard before and hadn't liked ... then or now. Or maybe it was the vibrations he could feel through his back, lying in the bottom of the boat that now had three inches of water in its hull. A heavy, steady growl, the thumping of dual diesel engines driving big propellers that easily pushed the large boat wherever its captain wanted to go.

Mike grabbed the side of the boat and went to pull himself up, but his back and shoulders cramped quickly and shot electric bolts of pain so severe he quickly let go and waited for the sensation to subside before he even dared to take a breath. He rolled over on his stomach, where he could push with his arms rather than pull, and slowly came up on his knees. He was not sure how long he had been out, but estimated it was now mid-morning. The skies were clear, the weather cool, and there was a good westerly breeze with small, soft rolling waves.

Slowly and carefully extending his arms, he untied one

of the gallon jugs of water as he searched the horizon for the motorboat. He raised the gallon jug, which was half full from rainwater, with both arms and swallowed a large mouthful. It burned as it went down his throat. He continued to hold the jug up, and his second and third mouthfuls went down much easier.

He spotted the boat coming down from the north. At least he thought it was the north. He couldn't see land anywhere and was guessing compass directions by the sun and what he imagined was the time of day. She was maybe 400 yards north and moving slower than he would expect anyone to go in these waters. Regardless how far he had drifted during the night, it wasn't like there was anything to see or any good fishing here; it was a place you had to go through in order to get to some place better. Like the airport in Atlanta.

The boat was a threat, but it could also be Mike's salvation. In the mild weather, with little other traffic around, it could very well be on auto-pilot. The captain could be downstairs, attending to guests or other issues, and the boat could run Mike over, probably without even noticing. His was a little boat and, especially without a sail up, easy to miss even under good weather conditions; he certainly wouldn't register on their radar. Mike was also just realizing that his boat was fairly swamped with rainwater from the prior evening and, even though the oncoming yacht was moving slow for her class, it would be hard for Mike to maneuver his boat if he happened to be on her course heading.

On the other hand, the motorboat represented everything that he needed: fresh water, maybe some supplies, but most of all, some idea of where the hell he was. As the yacht drew closer, he could hear the engines slow even more, and she seemed to alter course to stay just slightly west of him. Mike waved his arms, ignoring the pain from his back and shoulders, noticing the boat was even bigger than he had thought, maybe seventy feet total. It crossed his mind that these backwoods waters were a strange place for such a big and expensive yacht.

As the yacht slowed almost to an idle and came within fifty yards, a voice came over a loud speaker. "Captain of the small sailboat, are you in need of assistance?"

What does it look like, dumbass? I'm not doing my aerobics out here, he thought as he continued to wave his arms. The big boat approached to a distance Mike considered perilously close before turning hard to starboard, the stern drifting in Mike's direction and her bow facing into the wind. There was a loud metal clank, and two anchors that had to weigh fifty pounds each dropped from the bow and splashed to the shallow bottom in seconds. The boat engines stopped, and she floated back in the breeze, stopping about five feet short of the little sailboat. Mike was not a fan of most motor-boaters, but he couldn't help but be impressed by the parking job.

He sat down on the forward plank as a large launching platform opened away and downward from the back of the mammoth boat. Electric motors whirred, and the platform slowly lowered itself to the level of the waves. A swing gate at the transom opened from the back of the boat, and a woman in cutoff jeans and short blond hair stepped onto the platform.

"You get lost Detective?" Erin said with a smile on her face.

Mike sat looking up at her, speechless, thinking that maybe it was all a dream; maybe he was really having hallucinations from exposure, dehydration, or hypothermia. At least it was a nice hallucination.

"Even with your questionable seamanship skills, you should have made more distance since the last time we met," she said as she walked out to the edge of the platform and tossed him a rope.

Mike grabbed the rope but didn't say anything. He pulled the boat up to the platform and tied her up to a cleat. He looked Erin over from top to bottom, then looked up at the massive yacht, then back at Erin, but he said nothing. She looked cleaner than the last time he had seen her. She still had the remnants of bruising on her cheekbone, but the swelling was gone.

Erin was looking at the sailboat. "You took on some water… is there a leak?"

"No. Rainwater from last night," he responded, suddenly feeling very cold and starting to shiver from deep within.

Erin looked him over again and said, "You look like crap. Why don't you take a warm shower, and I'll take care of the boat."

She led the way, closing the transom gate behind them

as they walked onto the lower deck. She opened the sliding glass door into the main salon and walked through a narrow hallway, opening a door to a large cabin on the port side. "There's a shower through here. Use as much hot water as you want, but too hot and you're gonna make that sunburn worse. The towels and linens are clean; I washed them myself this morning. Sleep as long as you want; we'll stay anchored here till you get done."

He just looked at her, wondering if the whole crazy scenario was real. She looked at his burnt face and blistered hands, a slight shiver and lack of speech, and wondered if he might be even worse off than he looked. "Take off the dry suit … I want to make sure you can make it into the shower by yourself."

Mike was disgusted with the tremble in his hands as he went to unzip the torso of his dry suit. "Daa-a-mm-mn, you keeeep it cool-l-ld in heeere," he said as he shivered, finally pulling the zipper down past his waistline. He pulled his right hand through the tight wrist cuff, but when he tried to pull it through the rest of the sleeve, his back and shoulder cramped, and he grimaced in pain.

Erin said nothing but grabbed the sleeve, allowing Mike to pull his arm through with less pain. She helped the same way with the other arm. He sat down on the foot of the bed and groaned as he bent over and unzipped his beach booties and kicked them off. He took a breath and stood up in bent fashion, pulled the dry suit down to his ankles, and then stepped on it while he pulled one foot and then the other through the tight cuffs.

Standing in just his rugby shorts, Mike looked up wearily at Erin, took a deep breath, and said, "Thanks."

"Yeah, no problem," she responded, walking past him into the bathroom. She turned on the shower and, as she passed him again, handed him a bottle of water. "There is more bottled water under the sink; you need to work at drinking as much as you can. Like I said, sleep after you shower, and I'll take care of your boat." Mike nodded his head, then turned and walked to the bathroom. Erin closed the door to the cabin on the way out.

Although worried about her new guest, Erin quickly went to bridge and checked the yacht's controls. The anchors had held tight, and the big boat had not drifted a foot. There was still plenty of depth all around her, and the weather outside remained mild. She turned the radar on and watched for a minute until she was confident there was no traffic of any sort within a ten-mile radius, then turned it back off. She double-checked that the ship's beacon, the automatic identification system, was off.

She skipped down the stairs to the lower deck and out to the platform at the stern. She grabbed the swing-arm of the winch, normally used to launch jet-skis, and hooked the line up to the bow of Mike's boat. The boat was slowly and carefully pulled up at an angle onto the platform. Just as the stern of the boat came onto the platform, Erin stopped the winch, walked over to the little sailboat, and unscrewed the drain plug located in the transom. During the ten minutes it took to drain the water out of the boat, Erin surveyed the boat inside and out for any damage.

Finding none, she stepped back to look at the boat, seeming to hang there by a thread. She marveled at how small it was, and how far it had come. The only navigation equipment she had found was a sealed bag containing laminated charts and a compass.

She thought back just several nights prior, when she had been certain that she was about to be attacked by a large shark and this little boat rescued her. Steadfast was the word that came to mind when she looked at the boat; firm and unwavering in purpose and resolve. There were rough seas that night, but the boat had dipped her beam only enough to allow the swimmer on board, and then laughed at the waves banging at her boards. The boat had seemed to welcome Erin's hand on the tiller after Mike passed out. Erin thought back to the ghost Mike had been talking to that night. She recalled how the boat had almost steered herself to the beach, rolling over the surf break, and shaking her centerboard and rudder when bottom got close, letting Erin know she should lift them up to prevent damage. There wasn't much to her, but the boat was well designed and well built. Who knew what travails she had been put through as she struggled to safely bring her lunatic master wherever he wanted.

She got out a brush pole, hosed down the outside of the boat, and gave it a quick scrub. The boat had drained all the water out of its hull, and she replaced the drain plug, slowly lowering the winch so the boat rested on the platform leaning to starboard. She smiled at the boat and headed back to lower deck and then up to the galley.

From inside the refrigerator, Erin withdrew three lobsters she had caught and cooked first thing that morning. It was not lobster season, and she certainly didn't have a permit, but these were the least of the crimes she had committed in the past few days. She put a little bit of grapefruit juice and white wine vinegar into a bowl and added some chopped shallots and cherry tomatoes, some mustard and a dash of lime juice. She stirred the concoction vigorously, the aroma making her salivate as she anticipated one of her favorite dishes. She took the meat out of the lobster tails and cubed it, along with two avocados and some diced onion and bell peppers, threw it all in the bowl, swirling it around as her appetite grew. She emptied the mixture into the hollowed-out avocado halves and put three in the refrigerator, leaving the fourth on the counter as she took a healthy spoonful.

Mike leaned against the fiberglass wall with his head directly under the showerhead, the water slowly breaking away days of salt and sweat. The rugby shorts were rinsed repeatedly before being wrung out and hung over the shower door. He washed every part of his body as thoroughly as he had ever washed in his life, eventually sitting down to make sure he had washed every nook and cranny in his sea-wrinkled feet. The towel was soft and fluffy, but it still stung whenever he touched any of the many parts of his body that were sunburned. He looked under the sink and pulled out a plastic first aid kit, applying antibiotic cream to the blisters breaking through under the calluses on his hands.

He brushed his teeth, never thinking about who might have previously used the toothbrush, and only when he went to replace it did he wonder who owned it. Hell, who owned the whole ship? How the hell did this woman named Erin, who only a few days ago was bobbing for her life in the Gulf of Mexico, land up at the helm? And what was she doing in the brown water of Ten Thousand Islands? He rubbed the toothbrush against a bar of soap, worked it through the fibers, then rinsed it out and put it back where he found it, apologizing to whoever owned it for having so befouled it.

The air-conditioned cabin was cool and dark, the water-level portholes covered by closed curtains. Mike sat down on the bed with a towel wrapped around his waist. He didn't want to go to sleep until he had some answers about the ship he was on. He stared at the red numerals of a bedside clock indicating it was just past noon. He surrendered, let his head fall to the pillow, and barely pulled the sheet up before his eyes closed. He awoke an hour later, comfortable, like he was in his own bed at home. And then, suddenly, he was frightened, sitting up— he wasn't in his boat; what happened to his boat? It was dark and cold; where the hell was he? Where was his boat? As he moved, every muscle in his body seemed to start to cramp simultaneously, quickly reminding him of what he had been through and where he had landed up. He lay back down and, caught his breath, thinking to himself that the starkness of sobriety was gonna land up giving him a heart attack.

He pulled on his wet shorts, walked down the hall, through the salon, and into the afternoon sunshine of the lower deck. His boat was lying at an angle on the launching platform and Erin sat not far away, legs dangling in the water, a fishing pole in her hand.

Adjusting to the sunlight, Mike put his hand over his eyes. "Catch anything?" he asked.

She looked up. "Had a nice snapper on the line, but a goddamn shark cut him in half." Still looking up at him, she said, "You look better; guess you're gonna make it after all. I made some fresh lobster salad. You better help yourself before I eat it all." She wound in the fishing line and stood up. "Also found a bottle of Pedialyte, best thing for dehydration. Come on," she said as she walked past him, "you don't need to spend any extra time in the sun."

She motioned for him to sit at the table in the shade as she opened the sliding glass door and walked inside. She returned with a plate holding the three remaining avocado halves full of lobster salad in one hand, and two bottles of Perrier and a bottle of Pedialyte in the other. "The Pedialyte tastes like shit," she said, tossing him a fork. "Eat the lobster first; I caught it this morning up off of Marco." She grabbed one of the halves and started eating it, looking up at him only when she had a mouthful of her own. "Damn, I love this stuff."

"Thanks," he said, not sure what else to say as he took a forkful. She was right, it was delicious. As they ate, he looked at Erin fully for the first time. If she wasn't wearing the same cutoffs she'd worn the night he met her, they sure looked the same. She wore a long-sleeved cotton Guy Harvey fishing shirt that stopped right at her waist line. Her legs were tan and muscular, and her feet were bare. It was again her eyes that caught his attention, almost unnerved him. She was watching him as he looked her over. She didn't mind, didn't look away when they made eye contact—was it indifference? Self-confidence? Drugs? He never did get a straight answer on how she landed up bobbing around in the Gulf that night. He couldn't figure it out, but she was definitely different.

"Just you on this big ol' ship?" he asked.

"And you," she said matter-of-factly, adding, "Unless you brought along your invisible friend?" with raised eyebrows. They both knew what she was talking about, but Mike was not going to get into it.

"You own her?" Mike asked.

Erin thought about the answer for a while and simply responded, "Yeah, it's mine." She had another forkful of the salad, looking at him, assessing the man, while still enjoying her meal. "Be careful what questions you ask, Detective Kelly. You may not like the answers you get." Mike knew it was good advice; he had told many trainees never to ask a question to which they did not already know the answer. He wondered what her game was, what her background was, what she had been through that made her so different from anyone he had met.

"Well," Mike said, thinking about how to ask the question so that he learned what he needed to know, without her having to tell him something he didn't want to know, "just coincidence that you happened to pick me up?"

"Oh, hell no, I've been looking since yesterday. That's a tiny little boat, and this is a mighty big cesspool. Thought you would have made more progress south; assume you went into the islands and got lost?" Mike nodded his head yes.

"That morning on the beach, I went through your things and saw you didn't have squat for navigation—how do you think you're gonna make it through this area without a GPS?"

"Had one when I started," he said, recalling being run down by a boat with dual diesels just like this one. "Down at the bottom of Tampa Bay now; it's a long story."

"Yeah, well, anyway, I figured you might have some problems—seemed like a good chance to pay you back for helping me that night." They looked into each other's eyes, both wondering about all the things that weren't being said.

"Thank you; you sure showed up at the right time," Mike said.

"You're welcome," Erin responded, still looking at him, both being careful with their words.

"Can see you know your way around boats. That was a nice parking job when you picked me up."

"My daddy was a shrimper out of Pascagoula; grew up on his boats. He drank a lot, and I learned how to fix things when they broke, and how to drive when he was sleepy. Joined the Navy and got formal training as a marine mechanic. Haven't yet run into anything that floats that got the best of me." *She might consider the yacht hers,* Mike thought, *but there wasn't a chance in hell she owned it.* She could serve as a one-person crew for the beast, but she had never been around the type of money it took to buy a boat this size. The yacht was only four or five years old Mike estimated, probably worth close to two million. What the hell was she doing?

"That little boat you've got … ain't much to her, but she's a damn fine boat. Sits pretty in the water, even prettier in the rough stuff, and tougher than a mule. You build her?"

"No, my brother did," he responded, looking at the food, another topic taken off the table.

"Well, he did as good a job as I've ever seen." Mike looked up and smiled in genuine appreciation, but said nothing, not wanting the conversation to go any further in that direction.

"Where you headed to?" he asked, unable to suppress his curiosity. It was more than his reflexive law enforcement training; there was something about Erin that intrigued him, one of the few people he wanted to know better. Of course, there was almost certainly some criminal aspect to the story, and he couldn't help but try to figure it out.

"Why, you want to come along, Detective?" she asked, deflecting the question without hesitation and with a skill and confidence that continued to surprise him.

"No, I'm gonna finish the course," he said.

"That's what I figured. You know, the race—I'm sorry, the 'challenge', officially ends tomorrow. You've made it about two thirds of the way. Only way you're gonna make it in time for ceremonies is if I lend you one of my jet skis and a five gallon drum of gas."

Mike looked at her and smiled, liking the way she busted his balls. "Yeah, I know."

"Well, I can hang around for another day if you want to R&R—crash out in that comfy guest cabin."

"Appreciate the offer, but if I can just get my water jugs filled up, I'd like to finish this thing one way or the other."

"Figured that too," she said. "I already cleaned them old milk jugs out and put some fresh water in 'em." Mike smiled; he liked this girl.

"One thing, though," Mike said. "Been thinking about what you said about being careful about what questions I ask. You don't have to answer … but can you tell me what you were doing out there that night—the backstroke to Mexico thing?"

Erin looked at him without resentment, assessing him, weighing probabilities and consequences, guarded but unafraid. She tilted her head to the side. "Sooner or later, Mike, you'll lose your curiosity about things like that. Sometimes things just happen, there isn't any logic or meaning … it isn't good or bad, it's just life. But for now, are you asking as a cop or a friend?"

Mike also weighed his answer. He was a cop, there was no denying it. It was all he had ever done. But right now, he was mostly a lost sailor. "Friend," he said.

Erin breathed deeply. "Like I said, I'm a good marine mechanic. Do a lot of freelance work at a reasonable rate and don't ask too many questions. Had repaired a diesel fuel injector and agreed to go along with the owners for a check-out ride. They got high as hell and started talking about how they got this expert in concealed compartments, how much money they're gonna make bringing shit in from Colombia. Same time, they apparently forget I'm the mechanic that fixed their boat, start thinking I'm a whore, thinking they can buy me with enough money." Erin took a deep breath and looked up and to the left, recalling the incident of only a few nights prior.

"Well, they wouldn't take no for an answer—ain't the first time. Started to grab me and ripped off my shirt. I hit one of them good, hard as I could, but he was too high to go down, just started swinging at my head. They were pushing me up against the wall in one of the cabins, and there was a fire extinguisher mounted on the wall—like a gift. I cracked one of them in the head, and the other one goes crazy, pulls a gun out and puts it in my face. Kicked him hard enough between the legs to raise him up off the ground. I bolt for the door, and he starts shooting behind me. As soon as I hit open air, I jump into the water and start to swim ... that asshole still firing the gun into the water."

"You know the rest of the story; there was a squall line moving through, rough as hell. I'm a pretty good swimmer but had no idea where the hell I was. Next thing I know, you come sailing by talking to someone who ain't there and looking to bury your boat in the storm."

Mike looked at her but said nothing. She looked right back, no sadness, no regret, no remorse. Things happened; there wasn't always any logic or redeeming moral to the way things unfolded. He finished up the Pedialyte and groaned at the taste, washing it down with the last of the Perrier.

Well, he thought, I guess that explains the boat. I wonder what she's going to do with it. He had been in law enforcement all his life, and knew he was supposed to say something about going to the cops, prosecuting the two guys who tried to rape her. Convince her that, if she didn't help catch and prosecute these guys, they'd do it to some other girl. But he couldn't; he just didn't have it in him.

"Is there anything I can do to help?" is all he said.

She smiled. "You already did. You picked me up, remember? I've also charged about five grand to your credit card. If things work out, I should be able to pay you back within the month."

They both smiled, genuinely happy for the first time in a long time, so much understanding and meaning in words never spoken. "It's been a pleasure to meet you again, Erin. And you're right, the lobster salad was the best I've ever had."

"And it's been a pleasure to see you again, Detective Kelly. I hope you don't kill yourself. I think I'd like to get to know you."

Mike got up and walked down to the launch platform. Erin handed him a long-sleeved T-shirt, not unlike hers. "You gotta watch the sun; long-term effects are deadly," she said, chuckling. He put it on, pushed the boat off the platform, and stepped in.

"Oh, yeah," he said. "Where the fuck am I?"

"Where do you think you are?" she asked, laughing.

"Outside of Chokolosee Bay?" he said weakly.

"You're ten miles south of there … missed the first checkpoint. You're outside of Starter Bay."

Erin watched as he hoisted the sail and the little boat eagerly jumped to attention, heading southeast true and steady. "Hey, Sailor," she yelled as he checked his gear, "there's a GPS under your center plank—use it!"

XIV

The next two days passed without incident for Mike. He laughed at himself and his feeling of invincibility with his new GPS. How could this little machine make so much difference? Four little batteries somehow powering magical communications with sister machines in man-made orbs hovering 12,000 miles above earth ... was it even possible? Or was it simply the result of faith in a new mysticism known as science? Whatever it was, having the little machine tell him exactly where he was on the surface of planet Earth inspired confidence, a sense of knowledge and well-being, a feeling that he was headed in the right direction. He liked the feeling, and he thought of Erin every time he pulled it out and fired it up.

Erin had stored two additional gallon jugs of water, for a total of six, but he only had twenty miles to go before he rounded the southern tip of the Everglades and pulled into the last checkpoint of the race, at Flamingo. There was a shortcut, through Whitewater Bay, but he had seen enough of those inland waterways to last him a lifetime and, even with the GPS, he would be entering only under the direst of circumstances. Besides, he was not in a hurry. The adventure had been like a roller coaster ride and, right now, he was back to enjoying the ride.

A few hours after leaving Erin, he spied a sand beach and pulled the boat up before the sun went down. He sat on the center plank of his boat, looking out at the water and up at the stars, and thought maybe he was going mad—there was no angst, no desire for anything more, no concern about the next day—even the no-see-ums seemed to leave him at peace as the light breeze swept the smoke of the fire out over the waves.

He was up before sunrise, and the weather stayed fair. The movement of wind, known as a breeze, was something rarely noticed as you went about normal life, much less truly appreciated. It was an invisible thing, manifest only in its movement of other stuff, a leaf dancing sideways as it fell from a tree. A breeze meant nothing as you stormed along an interstate in a 2,000-pound mass of gasoline-powered steel. But all alone, in a small boat sitting atop hundreds of miles of ever-changing water, a breeze, and a sail to catch it in, meant all the difference in the world.

He pulled the sail on a beam reach, now heading due south until the point where he would round the southwest corner of the Everglades at Cape Sable and head almost due east toward Flamingo. He stretched the fingers in his hands, looking at the oars and thinking of the days he had spent laboring in the suffocating stillness. The blisters had busted and formed deeper calluses, ready for the next time they were called upon. But now the wind blew him along, and the boat skipped along the tops of the little waves, preferring the sounds of straining lumber to the creaking of oar locks.

He rounded Cape Sable and arrived at Flamingo well before evening. There was no sign of anyone associated with the EcoLoco challenge. Those who had finished were recovering and swapping stories down in the keys. Those who had surrendered, or broken down along the way, had long ago packed up their gear and headed back to wherever they came from, swearing to beat the challenge next year, or accepting the fact that this particular challenge was not meant for everyone.

Flamingo was a particularly crappy shanty town, even in its heyday. The area had been occupied by overly optimistic white folks since the 1890s, and there had been minor booms associated with prohibition, and again when rumors spread that Henry Flagler planned to build a railroad bridge to the Florida Keys. But dreams faded quickly to the reality of the oppressive heat, swarming mosquitoes, and the need to focus on survival in this hostile environment. Its inclusion as part of a National Park in 1947 had brought the area some status and tourism trade. Nowadays, folks came to camp, fish, and bird-watch during the more clement months, but no one would call it a popular destination.

Mike would have rented an air-conditioned hotel room

for the evening, but the park's lodge had been destroyed by a hurricane in 2005 and was never rebuilt; the closest lodging better than his boat was a fifty-mile drive on the only road in and out of Flamingo. So he tasted the water coming out of the hose by the fish cleaning table and made sure it was safe to drink. He rinsed out his jugs and filled them back up again. He pushed off and set back out to the mangroves farthest from shore, where the breeze tended to persist and the insects weren't as bad. It was his ninth night sleeping with his boat.

A direct sail across Florida Bay from Flamingo to Marathon Island in the Florida Keys was about twenty miles. But it was truly open water and, even with the confidence derived from his new GPS, Mike thought it a foolhardy proposition in a nine-foot boat. At sunrise he headed south by southwest, hoping to make land at Islamorada or one of the Keys just south. There were islands between him and his destination along this route, and these were not just mangroves, but real sand and coral Terra Firma Islands. In the event of bad weather or nightfall, he would be able to find relative safety on short notice at any of them.

He landed at the southern end of Islamorada well before sunset and tied up at the dock of the Islander Resort. The security guard took one look at Mike and the boat and forcefully told him in heavily accented Creole not to bother getting out of the boat. Shaking his hand as Mike secured the bowline, the guard said, "You not welcome here. Find someplace else." Mike lied and said he had reservations, which appeared to be a first for the guard, who was now not sure what to do. He pulled his personals bag out of the boat and climbed up the dock. With a big smile, he shook the guard's hand and said "Keep an eye on her. I'll be right back," walking off like he knew where he was going. He found the reception desk and rented a room for one hundred seventy-nine dollars with his remaining credit card. The young clerk gave him a parking tag to hang on his mirror, and he walked back to the boat and stuck it between the mast and the main halyard. He pushed a ten-dollar bill into the security guard's hand, saying, "Make sure there are no scratches when I get her back," and walked to his room.

The shower felt great and he longed to fall asleep in a real bed, but knew he should eat before he called it a day. There was an outdoor veranda that overlooked the bay and, out of habit, he requested a table on the far side, where his back would be to a wall and he had a good view of the other diners. The shrimp appetizer was overcooked, but the blackened grouper was fresh and perfectly prepared. It made him think of Erin, and he wondered what she was doing, mocking himself at the frequency with which he found himself thinking of her.

Another day and the trip would be done. Nothing had really changed, but somehow, everything seemed different. He sipped his beer and loitered over the fact that he had no pressing desire to get drunk. Eating was no longer a chore; he tasted and enjoyed the grouper, appreciating the spices, considering the effort that had gone into catching and preparing the fish. He saw the sun setting for the spectacle it was, perceived the breeze that no one else felt, knew the phase of the moon without looking.

What a strange journey it had been. He'd had a plan when he had started, but now he was happier without one. He had been run over, capsized, lost his gear, lost his way, sailed with porpoises, faced off with a raccoon, been sped out to sea in a lightning storm, found a girl bobbing in the ocean, had a gun pointed at his head, damn near died of dehydration, dined on fresh lobster in a magnificent yacht—and it would all be over in another day. What would happen when the adventure was over, when he returned to his job? Had anything really changed?

Was there a lesson to be learned? A revelation to be carried from this point forward? A way to make sense of the real world and enjoy his remaining days? He ate his grouper slowly, relaxed but still searching. He thought back to Erin's comments, about losing his curiosity, that things didn't always happen for logical reasons, didn't necessarily make sense, sometimes shit just happened. It reminded him of advice he had received somewhere along the way; he couldn't remember from whom or when, but basically, it was that some things were beyond your grasp, and trying to understand them only brought unhappiness. *Oh, yeah,* he thought, remembering one very important lesson, *you can only truly appreciate the value of a GPS when you have truly been lost.* He leaned back in his chair and watched the last of the sun melt into Florida Bay.

XV

Mike awoke on the eleventh day of his own personal EcoLoco challenge stiff and cold. The hotel bed had been soft, but he had grown accustomed to the bottom of his boat, and the curves of the memory foam stretched his relaxed joints and muscles in ways they were no longer used to. And while he had prayed for relief from the heat for over a week, he now found the conditioned air of the hotel room as cold as a freezer. He loved the toilet, however, and whispered his newfound affection to the adjacent roll sitting on the sink.

As he worked out the kinks in his joints and paid the bill, there was life in his steps. He hadn't resolved a single issue in his reflections the prior evening, but somehow felt like he knew something, just hadn't realized yet what it was that he knew. He apologized to the boat for leaving her alone the prior evening and felt bad as he fetched out three empty beer cans someone had thrown in her hull during the night. He checked and made sure his precious

GPS was still there, chiding himself for not bringing it in last night, but he didn't bother to turn it on as he didn't anticipate needing it on this, the final day.

The trip to Marathon Key was approximately twenty miles, and his plan was simple: parallel the western side of the Overseas Highway, also known as U.S. 1, as it wound its way through a narrow band of islands known worldwide as the Florida Keys. The dangerous parts would be the many cuts in between the islands on the way down, where cars soared across on concrete bridges, but little boats had to worry about tides, currents, fishing lines from the bridges, and bigger boats. The water on the west side was shallower and much safer than that on the east, but still deeper than most Mike had faced during the trip. The vortex of water being pushed through the cuts made each its own individual hazard, but none likely to be as strong as the force he felt at Port Charlotte.

By 1400 hours he saw a plane landing at an air strip running parallel to U.S. 1 and knew it was Marathon. He sailed into the first inlet past the airport and tied up at the Coconut Cay Resort where, nine days earlier, the first of the EcoLoco challengers had arrived to cheers of family and friends, and three days earlier, the last of official finishers had limped in burnt, sore, tired, and thirsty. No one was there to greet Mike now, but it didn't make a bit of difference. He climbed up three feet of dock ladder, sat back down on the dock, smiling as he looked at the little boat and said to her, "Well done."

He rented the cheapest room available and asked about

local rental car agents in case there was some deal he hadn't found on the Internet before he left; there wasn't. He called U-Haul, and they agreed to bring the smallest moving van they had down from Key Largo for a two hundred dollar surcharge. "Welcome to the Keys, and enjoy the view," Mike thought. "You'll be paying for it." He stripped down to his rugby shorts and went back down to the boat, pulling it up on the edge of the hotel's tiny man-made beach. He rinsed her off with a hose, tied down the sail, mast, and oars, and threw away all the remaining perishables. He held the GPS in his hand, still marveling at how he had failed to truly understand its value. *Trip's done,* he thought. *I have to remember to get you back to your owner.*

He bought some surf shorts and a T-shirt at the gift shop, then showered and changed. The van arrived at 10:00 am Wednesday morning. He loaded the boat in the back and pulled down the door. The drive back to Tampa took seven hours.

XVI

Mike wondered if his townhouse had stunk this bad before he left. He had noticed it immediately upon entering last night but was too tired to do anything about it. With the morning, it seemed even worse. After dropping off the van, he started to look for the source, but there didn't seem to be anything specific—the place just stank. He wasn't due back at the office until the following Monday and, although he had intended to go in earlier, he decided to do some cleaning first. What he thought would take a couple of hours landed up taking two days. It was still March, and the weather was good, so he started by opening every window in the house. There was an immediate improvement. He washed and vacuumed, he scrubbed and scoured. He got distracted from one job and started another but, after two days, he declared the place shipshape.

He scrubbed the boat inside and out, running his hands along her paint, looking for scratches or cracks; she had come through with no serious damage. He pulled her back to his shed, tilted her on end, and walked her inside. "I know it ain't as good as when you stayed with John, but it's all we got now. I promise I'll take you out as soon I get caught up at work." He put his hand on her side, patting her gently, and whispered "thank you" before he closed the shed door.

Monday morning came and Mike returned to the real world in the form of his job with Hillsborough Sheriff's Department. He had lasted two years as a Special Agent with the FBI. Worked at the Joint Terrorist Task Force, or JTTF, in Atlanta, handling counter-terrorist investigations. At first, he was excited at the thought of working against terrorists; the idea of preventing a terrorist attack incorporated the sum of all his professional hopes. But it took him less than six weeks to realize that every case he had been assigned was complete bullshit. They had all been thoroughly investigated, the suspects weren't terrorists, but you could never prove a negative, and rare was the supervisor willing to risk closing a case that somehow, no matter how remote the potential, might turn up having terrorist connections in the future. So the cases stayed open in perpetuity, handed down from one Agent to the next, the newest Agent getting the worst of the deal. The whole squad had only one case with any significant potential, but it would be years before he would be able to work on it, and he prayed hard that the country's premier law enforcement agency would be capable enough to wrap it up before then.

And it wasn't just that the cases remained open, but you had to come up with new and creative ways to make it look like you were making progress. Electronic surveillance taskings were initiated and then had to be justified every three months. It was more paperwork than Mike could have ever imagined, and no one had been arrested on genuine terrorist charges in Atlanta since the events of 9/11.

He had tried to transfer to another squad, but every Agent worth his salt was doing the same thing and he was at the bottom of the list. He took cyber courses, hoping to leverage a request for transfer to the squad that chased pedophiles on the Internet, but even though this was one of the least popular assignments, he was told he had to finish his time on the JTTF.

After eighteen months, he assessed that the entire Bureau had lost a sense of mission. Subsequent to 9/11, the focus on counterterrorism and associated domestic intelligence capabilities had become paramount, and the mission of catching the bad guys that state and local cops couldn't, fell by the side. Three months before John had been killed, Mike realized he had done more real work in one month as a deputy sheriff than he had in almost two years with the Bureau. With his state and federal experience, Hillsborough had welcomed him back at the rank of detective. He resigned from the Bureau with no fanfare and moved back to Tampa.

He enjoyed the work, especially the variety of his cases. There had been discussions of assigning him to the prestigious Major Violators squad, but it was agreed that this would cause dissension among the detectives who had worked their whole career within the Department. Instead, he had been happy with an assignment on the sleazier Vice/Morals squad, primarily trying to keep a lid on prostitution activity. His particular focus were teams that used prostitutes to target businessmen in town for conventions, but instead of getting laid, the men were robbed, extorted, and sometimes beaten. He had inherited cases on three prostitution teams upon arrival and had already arrested and filed multiple hard-sentence charges against the leader of one team, and developed an excellent source into one of the two other teams.

The work was rewarding. The businessmen weren't innocents, but neither did they deserve to be beaten and robbed for their indiscretions. The prostitutes were really the biggest victims, also frequently beaten by the gang leader if the plans didn't work out. Arresting one of the team leaders had genuine impact; it was good for the girls, good for the visiting businessmen, and good for the community.

But something big was missing, and it had made everything disoriented. All his life he had struggled to attain the "next level," to find that sweet spot where things worked like they were supposed to, where results corresponded to effort, where decisions bore consequences. He had moved from the County, to the State, to the premier law enforcement in the nation ... only to find it was all screwed up, no matter where you went. If anything, it got worse the farther you went up the line.

It was the goal, the next objective, the thing to strive for, that had been lost and left a big hole in his life. He had surrendered and accepted the fact that he had been pursuing something that was not attainable, that didn't exist. Maybe it was his surrender, which could perhaps be more candidly viewed as failure, that left the empty feeling in the pit of his stomach. In his need, he had considered returning to school and pursuing a PhD, but decided that this would only be a continuation of his folly. This is all there was ... it didn't get any better; get used to it.

And he was adjusting, was happy in the new job, finding satisfaction in his work, seeing his efforts resulting in bad guys being locked up and relatively honest folks being protected. It was all relative in the end; there was no state of ideal. Find your joy in what is, he had told himself, not what should be.

And then, on October 18th, almost six months ago, he had watched as his only brother, a better man in every regard than Mike could ever be, was slowly lowered into a hole. When they had taken the flag off the coffin and presented it to him, an irony so sad, so defiant of reason or meaning, everything he thought he knew came screaming apart, defying gravity and spinning off into dark spaces, raging against the very essence of life.

The drinking brought some solace, a dark numbness, but then he would wake up. His coworkers at the Department were sympathetic and covered his deteriorating performance. He somehow put one foot in front of the other ... but he wanted the misery to end.

XVII

Two weeks after finishing the EcoLoco challenge, returning home from work on a Thursday evening, Mike retrieved his mail from the community mailbox down the street from his townhouse. He didn't get many personal letters, and the handwritten address on one of the envelopes immediately caught his attention. He opened it as soon as walked in the door.

Mike,

Thank you again. Enclosed is a check for $7,842 to cover the charges I made on your credit card. Have also enclosed the credit card but, as you can see, I cut it in half because I don't trust our postal service. Actually, I have trust issues in general :)

I have bought a small marina down in Key Largo that needs a lot of work. If you need some exercise to get you *in shape for next year's "challenge," I could use some help and have a free room.*

Hope you are doing OK.

Erin

The check was drawn on a Key Largo bank, was in the name of Obduro Enterprises LLC, and was signed by Erin Shaw. From the check number, Mike figured it was the second check written on the account. He laughed as he looked at the cut-up credit card. He hadn't even received the bill yet. He wondered how she had gotten his home address, smiling at her resourcefulness.

Friday morning, he asked one of the clerks to run Erin's name through NCIC, the main national repository for criminal records. He doubted Erin had any criminal record, but you could never be too sure. If she did, he didn't want his name associated with the inquiry and had thus asked the clerk to make the inquiry, and he was going to have to pay a lot of attention to the charges made when his credit card bill arrived. A few hours later the clerk casually advised Mike that the query had come back negative. A review of the State's assets and property records confirmed that Erin had recently made a significant business purchase down in Key Largo.

Saturday morning 11 am Mike turned off U.S. 1 into a dusty gravel parking lot. There were two trucks in front of what appeared to be an old general store. To the left of the store was a typical Keys-style bungalow, so old that it still had individual air-conditioning units hanging from some of the windows, but with a large, newer, shaded deck on at least two sides. He parked next to the trucks and walked between the general store and the bungalow, and the marina immediately came into view. It was small, a covered open-air repair facility with a tin roof sitting directly behind the bungalow, and two wooden docks that could accommodate maybe two dozen boats behind the general store. Off to the right was a boat ramp and a wooden deck with a small Tiki hut that he presumed served as a bar.

He spotted Erin in the repair facility, talking to a man and pointing to various locations in the facility, the man taking notes as she talked. She was wearing cutoffs, and he wondered if she ever wore anything else. He watched for a minute, observing her comfortable but confident body language, the way she stood straight, feet firm, one hand on her hip and the other now pointing to the roof. She waited while the man took more notes, slightly pulling her ball cap up and wiping the sweat off her brow with the sleeve of her shirt.

He approached softly, but she turned quickly at the sound of footsteps on the gravel. She said nothing, but smiled and stared as he approached.

"Mango, this is Mike Kelly ... from Tampa," she said, as always choosing her words with care. "Mike, this is Billy Thompson, better known as Mango; he'll be overseeing some of the work I'm having done on the place." The two men shook hands and Mango turned to Erin, suggested that he had more than enough to start, and would have a crew at her site early Monday morning.

"You going to be with 'em, Mango?" she asked. "I don't like island time as much when I'm footing the bill."

"Yes ma'am, I'll be here. And you'll be happy with the work." Mango shook hands with Erin, nodded at Mike, and left in his truck.

"I'm gonna have a lift put in right here, and we'll have two dry stations right up there," Erin started explaining to Mike. "Two big ass fans up there," she said as she pointed at the far end of the tin roof, "so I don't stroke out in this friggin' heat." She wiped the sweat off her brow again.

She walked toward the docks and Mike followed. "The pilings are all good, but almost all of the lumber has to be replaced. Total of twenty slips if we don't crowd the entry to the repair shed."

She turned toward the general store. "Structure is fine; she could open for business tomorrow, but needs a lot of cleaning and prettying up, and some bait bins." Turning her gaze to the bungalow, she continued, "And that's my humble abode; not much to look at, but it's comfortable."

Mike nodded in appreciation. "Nice, but kind of a step down from the digs I last saw you in."

"Yeah, well … you know … you can't live like that for long; it'll make you soft," she said, smiling and dodging the issue. "Take care of this place and she'll take care of you for the rest of your life."

"You said you could use some help, what can I do?"

"You bring any tools, got any skills?" Erin asked.

Mike grinned sheepishly. "You didn't say anything about skills …"

Erin laughed and waved him to a closet at the front of the repair shed. "I still need to get my big tools down here from the panhandle, but I've got a few hand tools we can work with."

They carried the tools down to the far end of the southern dock in a wheelbarrow. Without saying anything, Erin jumped in the water and, one at a time, they replaced the stringers connecting one piling with the next, Mike working the high side, and Erin giving directions from down below. When they were done, she climbed up the dock ladder, sat on the dock and said, "I gotta get in better swimming shape if I'm gonna do much more of that."

She was looking off at the side of the property, still catching her breath, lacking any self-consciousness, unaware Mike was now staring and had stopped breathing. The wet T-shirt clung to her, and it was the first time he had seen the form and curves of her body. Her short hair, barely long enough to be pulled back behind her head in a bungee, was made darker by the moisture. Each droplet of water appeared reluctant to leave her skin; it seemed to Mike like something right out of a *Sports Illustrated Swimsuit Issue*. But it wasn't; she could bash your head in with a fire extinguisher, fix your dock, and leave you breathless without ever realizing it.

"I hope Mango is good to his word on those fans—this is a new type of hot down here," she said, now looking at the repair shed. Standing up, water still dripping off her, she walked over to the wheelbarrow. "I think the headers are good, but if we can pull the deck boards off today, hopefully we can get the composite down Monday."

She looked over at Mike, who was still staring. "You okay? Wanna take a water break?" He said he was fine, and they proceeded to strip the dock of the deck boards sitting on top of the headers. They finally took the water break when they finished the first dock, and then repeated the same process on the second dock.

By 6:00 pm they were done and sitting on her porch drinking cold Yuengling beer. Erin had shown him around the inside of the house, pointing out his bedroom and hers. While he went to get his overnight bag out of his jeep, she started her shower. After he had showered, he came out of the house buttoning his shirt and asking about where they were going for dinner. He looked up and it happened again. She was standing there in a white sundress with some type of light blue and yellow flower design, big brown eyes, sandals, a small purse in her hand, watching the sunset. She was beauty simplified to its core essence.

"Whoa, handsome … I said I'd buy dinner, but we aren't going to Mortons." She laughed. He was wearing jeans and a black shirt and was embarrassed by his own appearance and the fact that he had no idea what to say.

They ate dinner at a place called Flamingos, which, of course, led Mike to recount his brief visit to the ass-end of the Everglades of the same name. She asked about how the trip had gone after their last meeting, but there was really nothing worth recounting, according to Mike. They danced around issues as skillfully as Fred Astaire and Ginger Rogers, both having history they were not ready to discuss, and neither wanting to break the mood.

"Oh, I almost forgot," Mike said. "I have your GPS in my glove compartment, wanted to make sure I got it back to you. I didn't really use it that much, but it was weird how much difference it made just having it…"

"Yeah, kind of nice to be able to figure out where you are when you're all alone on the ocean. I gave it to you as a gift. I hope you'll keep it—you never know when you're gonna need it again."

It was like she knew things about him that he had never shared with anyone. "Thanks," he said.

The conversation stalled, and Mike was not as comfortable with the silence as Erin. "You said you were in the Navy?" he asked.

She hesitated, and he silently cursed himself for asking the question. "Shortly after high school," she said. "Was only in a few years but got some certifications and experience on big power plants that have really helped me a lot since then."

"Like it?" he asked, hoping this was more benign.

"Like the commercial said, it wasn't just a job … it was an adventure." She was looking at him, wondering where he was going, considering whether she should start knocking on his closet doors.

"You want to talk about your invisible friend?" she

asked, immediately sorry at the harshness of her tone.

"Nope," Mike immediately responded. He had tried too hard. The mood was broken. He really liked her, but he was just no good at this. "I'm sorry," he added.

She looked him in the eyes, assessing him and thinking. "Okay," she finally said. "Like the Arabs say, shwaya-shwaya, a little at a time." She continued, "The military can be a tough place for a woman; more so if you're arrogant enough to think you're the best engineman in the fleet. I can have a bit of an attitude, and I brought a lot of heat on myself for no good reason. Well, there's a lot of dark corners on a ship where you can get taught a lot of hard lessons. I learned my share—had to do it the hard way—but I struggled through and survived."

She took a deep breath. "And then I was below deck on the *Cole* when she was attacked. Not a scratch on me, but I was useless. Navy let me hang on for three months so I could get an honorable rather than general discharge. The psych issues were buried. Kind of a mixed bag, but that's the education of life."

Mike looked at her and wanted to say something comforting, something consoling, something wise. But he had nothing to offer, and she wasn't looking for anything. She looked back at him, watching and observing, but not judging.

"One day, you feel like it, you can tell me about your ghosts," she said. He nodded silently. She insisted on paying for dinner, and they drove back home to separate bedrooms.

He woke first Sunday morning, made coffee, and was sitting on the porch when she came out. Cutoffs again … at least he now knew she also had a dress.

"Ready for work, Boss," he volunteered.

"You got any religion?" she asked, a question so brutally direct it was hard not to sound offensive but somehow, when she asked, it wasn't.

"Catholic, why?" he asked.

"It's Sunday, dopey. I think I know where the Catholic mission church is … if you're interested?"

The Mass was in Spanish, and afterward, Mike said, "I think you got more out of that than me," referring to Erin's proficiency in Spanish, "but it was a lot nicer than the last time I heard you speak Spanish."

"You can never be sure who got what in deals like that. I once read about a seed uncovered during an archeological excavation that bloomed after being buried for 2,000 years."

"You're just a barrel of information," Mike said as they climbed in the jeep.

"Well then, if you don't mind, one more detour before we go home?" she asked.

They headed north twenty miles and then down a short coral-rock road, to what looked like an abandoned two-story building. There were fifteen to twenty people hanging around outside, mostly of brown complexion and mostly in the shade. Erin walked through the front door and hugged an old man who seemed to be in charge. "Rusty, this is Mike, a friend from Tampa," she said as the two shook hands. "What can we do today?" she asked.

In fifteen minutes they were back on the road with four bags of groceries and MapQuest instructions to four different locations. "It's a small world," Erin explained. "Rusty used to run with my dad, had a wild streak in him as long as any man I've ever known. If it was bad for you, Rusty wanted to try it. Never did anything in moderation. Went to rehab a half-dozen times, went to jail at least twice—think he did about four years. Then, all of sudden, he straightened up, got a regular job, and looked for opportunities to make amends. Second day I'm down here, I run into him at a supermarket, and he explains he's getting old produce for distribution to the poor, mostly immigrants. He can't speak a lick of Spanish and asks me if I could help. So he calls me if something urgent comes up; otherwise, I generally show up on Sunday morning and help however I can. Makes me feel good, and Rusty ain't the only one needs to build up some good karma points," she said, smiling.

By 3:00 pm they were done with deliveries. They picked up two pounds of boiled shrimp from the back of a restaurant and ate them on Erin's porch. Mike had suggested they get some work done, but Erin said there was always going to be more work to do; it was the time that was limited, and you had to make sure you spent some of that time resting and relaxing.

"You think you'll be coming back?" she asked.

"Yeah. I've really enjoyed it. Whole different view of the world down here. Assuming, that is, you have any interest in bunking a local cop with no tools and virtually no skills?"

"I like your company so far, Mike Kelly. And you've got skills, just not the same type as me," she said.

"One favor?" he asked, and she nodded her head, her mouth full of shrimp. "Seeing as this is a marina and all, I was wondering if I could bring my boat down here. I put her in my shed after the challenge, and it just didn't seem right."

"I would love to have that little boat down here. Something about her I fell in love with the moment I saw her... you know, beyond the fact that she saved my life," Erin said, laughing at herself. "Yeah, something about it..." she continued, "idea of her being down here just seems right."

Mike grabbed his bag, and they walked to his jeep. A dog was sitting in his passenger seat and although Mike had not seen him before, he assumed the dog belonged to Erin. "Not mine," Erin said, laughing, "but I damn sure like his attitude." The dog was maybe thirty pounds, black and white, nothing special to look at. Mike leaned over the driver's seat, trying to shoo him out of the vehicle, but the dog just slowly turned his head, pulled back an upper lip, and uttered a low growl. "Whoa, big boy, we're all friends here. But this vehicle is heading up to Tampa, and I'm sure you got friends here you'd miss." The dog turned his eyes back forward, totally disregarding Mike.

Erin came around the passenger's side and looked at the dog. "Come here, boy" she said, and the dog immediately jumped out and sat at her feet, looking up. She laughed and tossed him a peeled piece of shrimp she was about to eat.

"You're lying. I knew that was your dog," Mike said.

She laughed. "I rarely lie, and there is no way I would deny this dog if I owned him," she said, looking down at the dog. She bent over and petted him behind the ears. "Ah, hell, no tags."

Mike climbed in the jeep shaking his head. "Like I said, whole 'nother world down here." He headed out to U.S. 1, looking in his rearview mirror as Erin waved and then bent over to pet the dog.

XVIII

"Hey, you own a cellphone?" Mike asked as he climbed out of the jeep at Erin's place the following weekend.

"Some detective you are, can't even figure out a girl's phone number," Erin responded.

"Let me guess, a Walmart special? Just like all the dopers use?"

"Wrong. I prefer Target, better class of clientele," she said smiling. "And if the dopers are still doing it, it must work" she continued, Mike shaking his head.

"Well, I was just trying to be polite, make sure I was still welcome. I don't do good in awkward social situations."

"Trust me," she said "you'd know if you weren't welcome."

The mutt Mike had tried to shoo out of his car the prior week was now wagging his tail as he sniffed Mike's feet and legs. "Let me guess, he lives here now?"

"Vagrants and vagabonds," she said, "all trying to find

our way. C'mon, Jeep," she called to the dog and, as soon as he finished urinating on Mike's front tire, he came bounding up and walked by her side.

"Nice name" Mike said.

"I thought so too; picked it out himself," Erin responded, walking onto the porch.

Mike threw his bag in the bedroom. "What's the order of the day, Captain?" he asked, coming back out.

"Well, you seemed competent with a hammer and crowbar last week, so you get to pull up the bad wood on the Tiki deck. Rusty should be here soon; he's good with wood and, while I know it ain't worth the money and effort, there is some really pretty woodwork in the store I just can't stand to get rid of, so we're gonna try to clean it up. But first, let's take care of that boat hanging out the back of your jeep."

Mike had pushed the boat into the back of the jeep till it was right at the headrest. He had tied it up as best he could, but he had never been much good with knots. They carried the boat over to the front of the repair shed and laid her upside down on a small boat stand made of wood, the top of which was covered in outdoor carpet. "I made the stand just for her. I'm glad you brought her down," Erin said.

Mike ogled the recently installed boat lift and two fans as if he had some appreciation for their installation or capabilities. "Mango came through just like he said he would. Even fixed one of the roof panels that was loose and could have caused some real damage if it had fallen,"

Erin commented. Mike noticed a few boats already docked where they had been working the prior week.

A beat-up Toyota Corolla that had to be twenty years old pulled up in the driveway, and Jeep the dog went running out barking, his tail wagging and his ass wiggling in delight. Rusty stepped out, and Jeep jumped up on him, licking his hand and then nuzzling his head in between Rusty legs. Rusty laughed and petted the dog. "Helluva guard dog you got here, missy."

Mike estimated Rusty to be sixty-five years old, but it could be a lot less. The lines of his face, extending beyond a short and thin white beard, spoke of a life lived faster than the pace by which most clocks tick. He wore jeans that were worn thin and boots that had been repaired with silver duct tape. A plain white T-shirt over his torso, and a bent-up old straw cowboy hat made floppy and comfortable by years of sweat. His arms were thin but had a strength that could endure when stronger men wilted. He was wrapped in brown, tarnished, wrinkled old-man skin, the type that cut easily and would bleed without him ever realizing it.

"Good to see you again partner," he said as he shook Mike's hand and then gave Erin a hug.

Mike took his tools and started pulling up boards on the Tiki deck, making sure to carefully dispose of the nails as Erin had instructed. Jeep came out periodically to check on him, seeming to question whether Mike really knew what he was doing. He was just finishing around mid-afternoon as a thunderstorm came in from the east.

When he entered the general store, Rusty was busy working a noisy sander over the floors, while Erin was preoccupied working some wire wool on the more intricate built-in shelving. Mike recognized the wall wood as pine, a type of material he had always appreciated for its sturdy demeanor, but was typically only chosen where budget was the overriding factor. Erin set him to work with a can of paint stripper, a brush, and a wire wool pad, and pointed to the far end of the cabinetry without saying much on account of the noise screaming from the floor sander.

At some point, Mike noticed Erin had left, but Rusty was in his own world, watching what he was sanding like it would run away if he took his eyes off it for a second. Mike saw Erin through the back window with Mango, moving some big boxes, but kept to his assigned task.

Around 5:00 pm Erin pulled Rusty off the sander and announced it was quitting time. Mike thought to himself that, without the interruption, the old man would have continued through the night, never realizing the passage of time until the job was done.

"I had a thought about making some Sangria earlier this week," she said. "What do you guys think about burgers to go along with it for dinner?"

"Ah, hell no," Rusty spat out. "You gonna make some Sangria, you gotta have something worthwhile. We can run out on that fancy little boat of yours, pull up some Yellowtail, and be back this side of an hour." Erin smiled, and Rusty turned to Mike. "Come on boy, let's get outta here before she changes her mind."

Rusty picked up a net from behind the store, and the two hustled down to the docks. On the first toss of the net, he came up with what looked like mullet and threw them, net and all, in the back of a Seventeen-foot Boston Whaler Dauntless. Rusty jumped aboard the boat like he was seventeen years old, fussed at Mike for being slow, then fumbled around the console, commenting he had never driven the boat. He had the boat fired up and headed out the canal in minutes, turning the controls over to Mike but warning, "Don't crash it; she'll be mad as hell." He pointed out a general compass direction as he rigged up two poles and started cutting the bait, regularly looking up to check Mike's heading.

After fifteen minutes, he signaled for Mike to cut the engines. "Not allowed to drop anchor around here, and that means all you Yankees haven't fished this spot out yet," Rusty said, smiling. "We'll have dinner on board in no time." He threw some of the mullet in the water and then handed Mike a baited rod.

"One question," Rusty said as soon as the lines were out, and with an earnestness Mike had not previously seen, "you know where she get the money?"

"Wh-what?" Mike stammered, having no idea what Rusty was talking about.

"That marina ... this boat ... we're talking a lot of dough. I knew her daddy, she don't come from money. You don't look like you're no money either. She took something she shouldn't have, might not be too late to give it back." He was looking at Mike, and he could wait all day for the answer.

"No, Rusty, I don't know where she got the money— haven't really known her all that long."

"Well … maybe you don't know her long, but I can see you know her good. She's a good girl, but we all make mistakes. Ain't nothing truly good can come outta doing something bad. Trust me, learned the hard way. You find out, and I can help; jus' let me know."

Mike nodded his head, saying nothing. Within twenty minutes they had eight Yellowtail on board and were headed back home. At the dock, Rusty told Mike to bring the fish in to Erin and claim credit for catching all of them. "She likes a man can fish," Rusty said, back to smiling again. As Mike complied, Rusty pulled down a hose and washed the boat.

By the time Rusty got up to the porch, the fish were cleaned, and Erin was grilling them plain, with just a little olive oil and pepper, exactly the way Rusty preferred such fresh fish.

"You believe he tried to tell me he caught all these fish?" Erin said. "Hell, Fish and Wildlife coulda arrested him for what he did under the name of cleaning that first fish." Everyone laughing.

Mike tried to pour Rusty a glass of Sangria, and he signaled no with a hand over his glass. "Little girl over there will tell you, I've had more than my share of liquor and whatnot, but that was then, and nowadays I prefer a clear glass of water. Thank you though" he said, getting up and filling his glass from the kitchen faucet.

"Oh man, little girl, that was the best fish I ever had," Rusty said, leaning back and rubbing his stomach.

"Payment for services rendered ... I learned a lot about wood today," Erin said as she scraped the scraps into a dog bowl and added some kibble. They all watched contentedly as Jeep scarfed down his dinner, Mike and Erin having another glass of sangria.

Rusty said he had to get home before he fell asleep from the good meal, gave Erin a hug and shook Mike's hand. "You and that dog take good care of the girl," he said as he was leaving.

Mike cleaned up the dishes alone while Erin finished up something outside. After his shower, he found her in the kitchen, the dog sleeping at her feet, eating a slice of chocolate cake. She offered him some, and he passed. "Think I'm gonna hit the rack. I had a really good time today; thank you. And in case you didn't already know, Rusty is a helluva guy; you're lucky to have friends like that."

"Hmphh," Erin muttered, "that old man ... yeah, I guess he is all right," watching Mike walk down the hall to his bedroom.

He was sound asleep when he heard the door open quietly. He could tell from the dim backlight it was Erin, the dog right behind her. She closed the door, and the room went dark again, the wall AC humming. She said nothing, but he felt the sheet pulled back, then she was lying next to him, soft, warm, silent. Her hand found his erection and held it firmly as she mounted him, still not saying a word. He took in the curves of her body with the touch of a blind man, smelled the sun, tasted the salt off her skin. They switched positions twice, never saying anything, working as one. He proved himself better in bed than he was with tools.

When he woke, the sun was out, and Erin and Jeep were no longer in the room. He thought, for a moment, that it might have been a good dream, but her smell was on the pillow. He smiled and felt contentment; he was happy, perhaps as happy as he had ever been in his life.

Erin was out on the porch with Jeep, a cup of coffee, and the Sunday paper. He made himself a cup and sat beside her, feeling a little awkward but enjoying a sensation that was very new to him. She looked him up and down, but said nothing. Finally, he turned to her and said, "I want to tell you something."

"Oh, boy," Erin responded, rolling her eyes.

"My brother built that boat I was in," he said, his voice a little shaky. "He got blown up in Afghanistan last year." His voice shakier, saying words that had been bouncing around in his head for what seemed like years, but had never been spoken aloud. "He was the only family I had."

Looking down now, he continued, "I wasn't really right before he died ... and I've been a whole lot less since," his eyes welling up, hearing the words like someone else was saying them. "Well, I just wanted you to know that I'm more than a little banged up, and that's part of the reason... just wanted you to know..." still looking down, pushing the water away from his eyes.

Erin put her hand on his. "I know," she said softly. "You were talking to him that night on the boat." She waited a moment, scuffed his head, and said, "Come on, I know where they have a Mass in a language even you can understand."

The regular Catholic Church was twenty minutes farther away than the mission, and a whole lot whiter. It was early, and the crowd was small. Erin watched Mike for cues on when to sit, kneel, or stand, finding the proceedings a bit overcomplicated.

Afterward, Rusty had a half-dozen bags of groceries ready for delivery but said he was also looking for some extra help. "Little kid got burned pretty bad last year. He's doing all right, but has to go up to the burn center at Jackson Memorial every few months for some kind of treatment. Him and his mother had a ride all set up, but the ride got arrested last night, threw a wrench in the plans," Rusty said, letting the comment hang in the air.

"I can take 'em myself," he continued, "but it won't be till late; work here won't be finished till this evenin'."

"I can do it," Mike said. "After we deliver the groceries. I'm headed up to Tampa and Miami ain't that far out of the way."

"That's what I was hoping you'd say, boy. Jus' couldn't bring myself to ask for some reason," Rusty said, patting Mike on the back. "Here's the address; think you can pick 'em up sometime before 5:00?"

"No problem," Mike answered, conflicted by the new

sensation he got from helping people and his desire to spend as much time as he could with Erin.

The deliveries rolled by, Erin talking about her plans for the marina and showing a business acumen that Mike had overlooked. "We already got monthly rental on four of the slips and commitments for another six starting next week. We coulda had more, my rates are the best in the area, but I want people who are gonna pay regularly, don't want be in the collections game. That'll be half full, and I need another five to be viable. But once them boats are there, their owners gonna be coming through the store, and that's where I'll make my profit. Bump up the margins just enough on everything in there, the price of convenience. And we get that Tiki Bar going on the weekend and it'll be nothing but profit."

It was the most Mike had ever heard her talk, and he listened in rapt attention, wondering how she had acquired such a wide span of knowledge. It was almost like she tried to conceal how smart she was, and it was only when she was immersed in an issue, essentially talking to herself, that she revealed the breadth and depth of her understanding. He thought of his own academic career, how he had considered pursuing a doctorate degree but, outside of technical law enforcement issues, he doubted there was anything he knew that she didn't know better. Hell, the issue of cop work hadn't come up, maybe she even knew more about that.

After the deliveries, they returned to Erin's house, but there was little time left before he had promised to bring the family up to Miami. In the moments he had not been mesmerized by Erin discussing her business plans, his mind had returned to the night before, and he longed to feel her again, knowing he would better appreciate what was going on. But instead, he walked out to the jeep and threw his bag in the back. Erin reached up and kissed him on the lips. It was their first kiss, a kiss for the daylight, a kiss of sincerity and affection. It was short, but it felt almost as good as the night before.

"You coming back next weekend?" she asked, standing in her cutoffs and T-shirt, maybe showing a girly side he had not seen before.

"Wouldn't miss it for the world," he said, climbing into the jeep and warning the dog to take good care of the girl.

XIX

He arrived at the family's house just before 5:00 pm. The mother and son were sitting outside under a tree with a small overnight bag. She looked to be forty years old, with hard black hair and tired brown eyes. The kid couldn't have been more than eight or nine, happy and carefree, the way kids are supposed to be. One of his ears was mostly missing, and there were obvious skin graft scars on the same side of his face and throat. He wore shorts, and one of his thighs was covered in clean white bandages.

The boy helped his mother into the front seat and then scampered into the back. The mother and son spoke to each other in Spanish, and then the kid said, "My mother said to say thank you for being so kind to strangers and that Mr. Rusty is an angel of the Lord."

Mike chuckled. "Well, tell your mother she is welcome; it is really right on my way ... but I'm not so sure about Mr. Rusty being an angel." The kid laughed and then spoke to his mother, who concealed a giggle.

As they drove over the bridges of the Florida Keys, the kid asked questions freely and rapidly, ignorant of social decorum, free of the secret bonds that restrained inquiries among grown-ups. Once the kid found out Mike was a cop, the pace of questions increased. When he found out Mike had also been an FBI Agent, they came like the roar of a machine gun.

After an hour the kid slowed, his mother sound asleep in the front seat. Mike asked what the kid was going to do at the hospital. "They're gonna try to put on my ear" he said, "they are growing it here, under my bandage." It was said so matter-of-factly it took a few seconds to sink in. Mike looked at the kid in the mirror; he was looking off at the water, the question asked, answered and done.

"Does that hurt a lot?" Mike asked.

"I dunno, never done it before," the kid again looking off at something in the water. No fear, no pity, no concerns, no regrets.

By the time they hit Homestead, the kid was also asleep. In the evenings this time of year, the weather was still pleasant, and the wind whipped through the jeep as they headed up the turnpike extension toward Miami. Going seventy mph with a cool breeze, the lights twinkling in the darkness off the east side of the turnpike, Miami could appear a comfortable place to live. But Mike knew better, knew the dangers that lurked in the dark, the hardness that had taken hold of the city decades before, when the cocaine money came in and robbed the city of all civility and charm. Off to the west was a hundred miles of thick Everglades, full of different dangers that he had only recently become acquainted with. Between the two, Mike figured his preference would be the Everglades, where you generally knew which animals were trying to kill you.

He pulled out the red-lens flashlight he always kept in the glove box and looked at the directions Rusty had provided. He turned off the turnpike onto the Dolphin Expressway and headed east toward downtown Miami. Continuing to follow the instructions, he exited the expressway south on NW 17th Avenue and, in three blocks, turned into the parking lot of a seedy hotel inhabited by enough shadows that he opened the glove box again, pulled out his Glock, and tucked it under his thigh. He slowed enough to see someone passed out near the entrance and another shadow looking for something they could undoubtedly be arrested for.

Mike rolled out of the parking lot a little faster than he rolled in, and headed south again on 17th Ave. He turned west on Flager St., through Little Havana, and the south on Red Road. In 15 minutes they arrived at the Biltmore, one of the oldest hotels in the area and one of the last vestiges of how rich people had lived back in the old days of Miami. As he parked the car, the woman awoke, groggy but startled, looking around, finally looking at him and remembering where she was and how she had gotten there. She quickly looked back outside the jeep and then looked at Mike, waving her finger, indicating this was definitely not her destination. She woke the kid, who rubbed his eyes and listened as she spoke. The kid looked around and immediately understood what his mother had been saying. "The directions must have been wrong; this isn't our hotel."

Without further explanation, Mike told the kid he had to run inside and he'd be right back. The kid nodded his understanding and translated to his mother. Inside, Mike showed his badge and said he needed to book a room for two friends who were very important to him. He provided his credit card and explained that he wanted the mother and kid well taken care of and all expenses put on his credit card. That was the advantage of a place like the Biltmore, they still remembered how service was supposed to be. The clerk called the bellboy, a man of sixty years with strong arms and soft eyes, handed him the key, and provided him stern instructions in Spanish. "Everything will be taken care of Mr. Kelly, you have my promise," said the clerk. She handed Mike a business card and continued, "It has my desk and cell numbers on it; if there is anything else you need, or you want to check on your friends, please don't hesitate to call me."

The bellboy accompanied Mike out to the jeep. The woman and kid watched but said nothing. "Your hotel had a fire this morning and is closed; you'll be staying here, but everything is paid for," Mike said. Apparently the woman spoke more English than she let on, because she immediately began speaking to the boy and voicing her disapproval. The kid, also confused, started to relay his mother's concerns. "She says we can't afford ... we can't stay at anyplace like this—" But the bellboy interrupted in Spanish. Mike had no idea what he was saying, but he spoke to them in a voice rich with authority and experience, and they listened. He opened the door for the mother, grabbed the bag from the kid, and started to escort them up to their room.

The mother looked back over her shoulder and then said something to the kid. "Thank you," the kid said to Mike. "My mom said thank you very much."

He looked at the kid, now fully awake and eager to get to his hotel room. "You're welcome," Mike said, wanting to say more. "Hey, kid, what's your name?"

"Ernesto," the kid answered.

"What's your last name?"

"Obduro," the kid answered.

"Good luck tomorrow, Ernesto!" The kid said thanks again and then walked with his mother into the aging but still graceful hotel.

Mike climbed into the jeep and drove the remaining four hours back to his house in Tampa.

XX

The pattern followed for three months, Mike driving down on Friday night unless he had pressing case activity. Business grew quickly. Erin had stocked the store and hired a local girl to staff it most of the open hours. Almost all of the slips were rented out, and she had started to get some repair work that she handled by herself. With the growing business, there was less time to spend together, but there was enough, and he found a strange satisfaction in just being there, being around Erin, helping out however he could.

With the uptick in business, Erin had been forced to forgo their Sunday mornings together, but begged Mike to go to Mass without her and continue to help Rusty deliver groceries. It was much better with her, but he found himself also enjoying these mornings alone. He started taking Jeep the dog, who behaved better than most people Mike knew, and acted as if it were providentially ordained that he should be sitting in the front seat, riding around with Mike.

He extended his visits with Rusty, picking up odd chores and listening to stories when things were slow. Rusty talked about his days in jail, his days in rehab, all the mistakes he had made along the way, never seeming to embellish or be embarrassed. "It was what it was, and it is what it is," he would say with a shrug of his shoulders. Mike had assumed that everyone like Rusty harbored general resentment toward cops, but he believed Rusty when he said that he was grateful for everything that had happened in his life, including getting busted and going to jail; it had landed him where he was, doing good and feeling good.

Things had also started to change in Mike's perspective of the world. Maybe it was going back to Mass, or maybe it was being around people like Erin and Rusty. His need for a goal, an objective to be conquered, seemed to diminish with every visit to the Keys. He found himself sometimes eating dinner with Erin and realizing that he was thinking of nothing else. He would listen to her talk, or watch her eat, and that was all he wanted. It was a contentment he had never known.

He had always wanted to be a policeman, catching bad guys, protecting innocents. He had always been aware of an evil force in the world. He could not name it, put a finger on it, but it was there, and it was his job to keep it in check. But now, instead of contemplating the source of evil, he had begun to wonder what made people do good things, even noble things. What prompted a person to sacrifice for another, a stranger who probably didn't deserve the help? Were Rusty's actions just amends for past misdeeds, atonement made out of fear as death inevitably crept closer? Or was it something more, some mystical force that pushed people into helping each other and then rewarded them with sentiments of satisfaction and contentment, like a treat given to a dog who obeyed his master's command?

Mike had recently been thinking about one of the homilies he had heard at Mass weeks prior. The priest had not said God was manifest in love, but that He actually was love. Mike had never heard the theory but, as he struggled with the interpretation, he found it a comfortable thought that there was a God, and He was among us everywhere, tangible in every act of love, rewarding us for such acts and leaving bread crumbs to the trail of happiness. And the more he thought about the God of Christians, the more it seemed appropriate that their king had set such a great example of love, hanging on a cross to give a get-out-of-jail-free card to a bunch of assholes that were killing him.

Mike was acutely aware of his reflections, of the time he spent thinking about these things, but he kept it all inside his head. You never knew how things were gonna turn out, better to keep it to yourself ... who knew what might change if the thoughts were given voice.

XXI

Mike had been conducting an interview on a Thursday afternoon when he received a phone call and let it go to voicemail. As soon as he was done he looked at his phone, saw the missed call was from Erin, and dialed up his voicemail. From the very first word, he knew something was wrong. She had tried her best to deliver the message in a casual tone, tried to minimize the significance, but it was his immediate instinct that she was lying. She had said all was well, but she had to head up to Miami Friday night for a Saturday morning meeting regarding some needed additional financing. She wasn't sure when she'd get back, probably not till Sunday, so there wasn't any sense in his coming down for the weekend. Unless, of course, she had said, he was really coming to see Rusty and Jeep these days. Trying to inject some levity. She promised to call back Friday, when she had things confirmed. He didn't let himself wait and called her back as soon as the message ended. No answer.

In the milliseconds it took for his mind to start wandering, his stomach flipped, and he looked around for something to throw up in. It was the surprise that caused the physical reaction. If you were ready for something, you could control your responses. But this was like a lightning bolt out of a clear blue sky—the possibility hadn't even crossed his mind. His forehead was cold yet sweaty, and he knew it was too late to control his physiology or his appearance. He ducked into the men's room and sat in a stall, buying some time to get his stuff together. Deep breaths, he told himself, pull it together; you've been through worse. He was already trying to mentally stop the bleeding and cauterize the wound. It's just a girl; you haven't even known her a year; you'll be over it in a week. And while he wouldn't dare let himself think it, somewhere buried deep inside, he knew the slippery, sideways disorientation was exactly what he had felt when he was told of his brother's death. Deep breaths he kept telling himself.

When the physical reactions subsided, he rinsed his face with cold water and dried it with some paper towels. He had been doing well in the months since he met Erin, but people had seen his fall after John's funeral and were still watching him; appearances were important. He went to the captain's office and asked if it would be problem to take off Friday, volunteering that his cases were all squared away and no significant activity was expected over the weekend.

Captain Derek Grant looked up from the report he was

reading and, peering over his glasses, gave Mike a hard look. He was not afraid of the silence and let it hang in the air, seeing if it might compel the detective to volunteer anything else.

"You know better than me if you can go," he said, "and if you shouldn't be going, I'll find out about it sooner or later."

"Thanks, Cap," Mike said, and he hustled down the stairwell and out the side door to the parking lot to avoid having to talk to anyone else.

He overcame the temptation to buy a bottle on the way home, knowing the welcome comfort and sleep it would inevitably bring, but afraid of where it would lead, what would happen when he awoke and the numbness was gone. The night was long and sleepless and, one by one, the demons he thought he had conquered slowly made their way back home in the dark, laughing and gluttonous.

He was showered, dressed, and out the door by 5:30 Friday morning. The day was bright and crisp, a fair wind blowing in from the Gulf. But if the night was long, the drive from Tampa to Key Largo seemed a torment without end, each slowly passing mile a mere step down an eternally spiraling path of pain and self-doubt.

As a coping mechanism, he tried to distance himself from events, to look at what was happening with the cold objectivity of a criminal investigation. There was absolutely no proof, he told himself, that there was anything wrong. Forget proof, there was not even any circumstantial evidence to suggest that any of his concerns were justified. Erin had made a call indicating she had to attend to business over the weekend. Every word was plausible and there was no logical reason to assume otherwise; but Mike similarly had absolutely no doubt that his instinct was right, and that everything had somehow gone wrong.

But where had it gone wrong? The more he tried to objectively answer this question, the more it became obvious that things had never been "right." He had met the girl when he was too drunk to sail a little boat and she was bobbing in the sea about to be eaten by sharks. These circumstances don't happen to normal people; things were broken from the very beginning.

"It felt right," he told himself. "It felt ... perfect."

"Yes," the demons answered back, "and when you're lost at sea on a raft, a little sandy island looks like paradise. But soon you realize there is no water, no food, and now you're not even moving toward a safe haven ... you're even more broken than you were on that little boat. To a rat, a turd looks like a smorgasbord, but it isn't—it's just a turd."

It was a keen observation and hard to argue against. There was no doubt he was a broken man when he met Erin. But he was just as confident that he had felt genuine love, he was as sure of this as he was that she was lying when she left the voicemail.

So where did it go wrong? he asked himself again.

"Where did it go wrong? Really, jackass? I'll tell you," the demons answered back. "You think it's just a coincidence that she was too busy to spend Sundays with you? You really think you're that much fun to be around? Did you ever work at the relationship? Did you ever think about what she was looking for? Shit, the two of you had more secrets from each other than you did shared experiences! The real question is how the hell it lasted as long as it did, and how you didn't see it coming to a crashing end like the rest of us!"

The secrets. Mike didn't really think of them as secrets. When someone asked for information and you concealed that information, that was a secret. There were certain things they had not talked about, things that perhaps they were not proud of, or that would hurt to discuss, but it wasn't like either of them was trying to conceal the existence of these issues. It had seemed to Mike, at the time, that they had an unspoken agreement not to pry into such delicate matters. When one or the other wanted to bring it up, they would start the conversation.

But maybe he had misunderstood. His communication with Erin was indeed different from anyone else he had ever met. In reflection, it was close to how he had communicated with John, both often knowing what the other was thinking, but keenly aware that uttering the words could give life to bad things that had not yet been born, and the pain caused by a single spoken word could never be taken back, no matter how many words of regret and sorrow might follow.

"You are an idiot, plain and simple," the biggest demon said. "You actually believe that girl could know what you are holding back, that she could read your twisted and warped mind? If she had any inkling of how the few alcohol-soaked brain cells you own worked, she would have swum into the shark's mouth rather than get into that boat with you."

Another valid point, Mike conceded. So I should have talked more, tried to communicate better?

"No dipstick, the more you communicate, the more she realizes how screwed up you are. You did the right thing and rode the pony for as long as you could; but sooner or later she was bound to realize you're a loser who can't hold a job for more than a couple of years, has no idea of what he wants from life, and cries when he gets drunk."

Shit, that last one hurt.

The big hairy guy in the back of his mind was right, he was a loser. But his mind drifted back to some of his conversations with Erin, and the one thing he was sure of, was that he had been a good listener. He could recall the specific words she had said at almost any time they had been together. He listened hard, in rapt attention, to every syllable that fell from her mouth. He had taught himself to be a good listener when it came to interviewing suspects and witnesses, but with Erin, his focus came naturally, watching her lips move as he listened to her words like the lyrics to a favorite song. They may not have had many long conversations, and there were certainly conversations that had been avoided, but he had heard and understood everything she had said. He had also understood what she hadn't said.

And in all that time, he had never once suspected that her words, or anything else she did, were intended to conceal or mislead. And though he might be a loser, there were some things he was good at, and there were some things that were true. And in his whole life, he had never once been wrong about what was true, and never backed down from facing it. And that was why he was driving to Key Largo. They'd find out soon enough. The demons chortled but said nothing.

XXII

He pulled the jeep into the sandy parking lot and immediately spotted her standing on the patio of the small bungalow. She turned around at the sound of his car and looked directly at him. She was wearing the cotton sundress with blue and coral flowers, standing firm, arms crossed across her chest, and then one hand reaching up to cover her mouth.

He turned the engine off, and they sat there staring at each other, both wondering what was going to happen next. She unfolded her arms and started to walk toward the car, a walk and disposition Mike had not seen before. She held up her hand, motioning for him not to get out of the car, upset.

"Goddammit, Mike, I told you not to come. What are you doing here?" He was still in the car. Her voice was nothing he had ever heard before and he was stunned. She was angry, but more than angry; he thought she might be crying.

"Don't even get out!" she said firmly, but with a quiver in her voice. She looked away from his face, maybe looking at the door mirror, avoiding eye contact. But her voice was emphatic. "I mean it, Mike! I told you not to come. Get the fuck out of here and go back home."

He put his hand on the door handle. He wanted to run to her, to hold her. But he had no idea what was going on. He quickly scanned the property, looking for another man, looking for some clue as to what was going on. Why wasn't she wearing her cutoffs? Where was Jeep?

"Do not get out of the car!" she yelled. She was crying. "Can't you understand what I'm saying ... get the fuck out of here ... I do not want to see you!" She was looking away but pointing at U.S. 1. "Just go—leave now."

He sat there, looking at her, completely lost and wanting nothing more than to fix whatever he had done wrong. "Oh, this is even better than we thought it would be," the big demon said with glee. "Why don't you rush into the house and find her new boyfriend with his pants down!" Tears began to fall from Mike's eyes as the demon continued, "C'mon, cry baby, be a man; go settle this shit right now!"

Mike sat there looking at Erin, as lost as he had ever been in his life, and she refused to look at him. He turned the engine over, put the jeep in reverse, and backed out the same way he had come in.

XXIII

U.S. 1 is a divided highway, with a one hundred-foot patch of grass and gravel separating north and southbound traffic. Mike was forced to turn right coming out of the parking lot, traveling south but headed nowhere. Deep breaths he told himself. But while he had not known what was going to happen, he had been mentally prepared for anything, and was able to control his physiological reactions as a result.

He didn't make a U-turn at the first divide in the highway but continued south, pulling into the parking lot of a liquor store five minutes later. As he walked to the store's front door, his mind was humming like an overworked transformer, and yet it was almost like he was not thinking at all. He pulled hard on the door and was surprised when it did not spring open. He stepped back and noticed it was dark inside. He looked around, still not comprehending, then he looked inside again. It finally dawned on him that it was still mid-morning. He looked at the sign with the hours of operation and realized the establishment would not be opening for another hour. As he walked back to his car, he got the feeling that he was missing something. He stopped and checked his watch, looked back at the store, then got in his car and headed south again. Surely, he thought, there had to be someplace nearby that catered to the needs of local drunks.

Ten minutes later, he pulled into another empty parking lot, this time on the other side of the highway. He walked to the front door again, put his hand to his forehead to read the opening hour, and was once more disappointed. He stood on the step of the building for a moment, considering whether he should just wait in the car or continue the hunt. He decided on the latter and, as he reflexively crossed the median returning to his southward trajectory, he noticed the vehicle pulling out of a nearby store and also turning southward. He noticed it on a level that was below consciousness, below true perception, and although, later on, he would not know exactly where he had seen the car, he would know that he had seen it before.

Ten more minutes south, Mike pulled into Little Willie's Bar & Grill, which was opening for lunch. He sat at the bar and ordered a double of Jameson Whiskey and a Budweiser. The bartender looked at him twice but said nothing. Mike was not in a hurry and sipped the whiskey, enjoying the feel as it slid down his throat. He took in the rest of the bar as he took his first gulp of the beer. It was a dump and he was the only customer. *Nice to be home,* he thought.

On his third round, a drunk who had stumbled in from the morning daylight a few minutes prior was sitting next to Mike and asking for a few spare dollars. The bartender watched out of the corner of his eye as Mike slid the guy a twenty and told him to enjoy. A few rounds later, Mike wandered back to the bathroom and was in full stream when the bum came in. For a drunk, he was pretty fast; the filet knife was inside of Mike's shirt and pressing against his back before he could stop pissing.

"You want to keep your guts on the inside, just stay still and don't make any sudden moves," the guy said as he lifted the wallet out of Mike's back pocket.

It was too much to take, but Mike couldn't summon up the energy to do anything about it. Maybe it was fate that he should bleed to death on the dark, piss-soaked floor of this shithole. *Just do it,* he thought to himself, still holding his pecker in his right hand. *Do it, and let's be done.*

The door of the bathroom creaked as it opened and, whoever it was, they were apparently quicker than the drunk. As Mike stood there with his dick in his hand, he heard a quick swishing sound followed by a solid thud, and then the drunk staggered and crumbled onto the floor. Not a word said, Mike tucked himself back into his pants and turned to see Rusty standing there with a small leather blackjack in his right hand. Mike looked down at the drunk lying still on the floor and back up at Rusty, who was slipping the blackjack into the back of his pants.

Rusty bent over and pulled the wallet out of the drunk's hand and tossed it to Mike.

"Some cop you are. I hope you're better when you're sober. Let's go," Rusty said as he turned and headed out of the bathroom. Mike followed, still not having said a single word. Rusty nodded at the bartender on the way out. "He'll be okay, but someone needs to clean him off the floor; owe you one."

Mike continued to follow as Rusty exited the building through a side door Mike had not noticed. Rusty said something in Spanish to a woman in the parking lot. Mike tried to pierce the haze caused by the opposing forces of whiskey and bright sunlight; it was the mother of the burnt kid, she was wearing a dishwasher's apron. "Give me your keys," Rusty said quietly and, when Mike complied, he tossed them to the woman and spoke some more in Spanish.

"Pretty good timing back there in the bathroom,"Mike said as they pulled onto U.S. 1 and headed to Rusty's house. Rusty nodded his head slightly but said nothing.

They pulled under the tree in the front yard and walked into the house. "Have a seat," Rusty said, motioning toward the kitchen table. He pulled a plastic container out of the refrigerator and put half of the contents into a bowl. He put the bowl in the microwave and set the timer for a minute, then turned around and looked at Mike without saying anything. The silence was as bright and overbearing as sunrise reflecting off a flat Florida bay.

He put the bowl in front of Mike along with a glass of water and some hot sauce. "Chicken with rice and beans. It's delicious just as it is, but sometimes you need the Tabasco when you've lost your taste. There's a bunk in there," Rusty said, pointing to the first door in the hall leading out of the kitchen. "Sleep it off after you finish. I've got to go, but Maria will have someone drop your car off, probably before you wake up."

He continued to look at Mike. But his eyes reflected no judgment, betrayed no plans for lectures about lessons learned and moving forward. His eyes … green and brown? Or maybe aged into gray like the whiskers on his face? They just observed, perhaps with empathy, yet always with a clarity that came only with age. They saw neither the past nor the future, only the present.

"She said she didn't want to see me again."

"You can't control other people," Rusty said quietly. "Hell, most of us can't even control our own selves."

"You look like your lookin' for advice, so this is what I'll tell ya: Ain't no good gonna come from you hanging around here. Get back home, get to work, stay busy, get into a routine, and start praying for help. Be good and be patient, and sometimes—not always, but sometimes—things have a way of working themselves out. That's all I got."

Rusty headed for the front door. "What about my boat?" Mike shouted.

"Last thing you need in this type of storm is that boat and the history that goes with her. I'll see to her. If you want, I'll bring her up to you after a while." The door closed, and the truck engine started and faded away. Mike slowly processed half the bowl of food with a few slugs of water, walked down the hall, kicked off his shoes, and passed out on the bunk.

XXIV

Mike woke up at 3:00 pm. The house was quiet except for the branches of an old banyan tree brushing against the roof. He put on his shoes and walked to the front porch. His jeep was under the tree, and he found the keys under the seat. He cranked the engine and sat back in the driver's seat, considering whether to head north or south.

He put the jeep in gear and headed toward the marina. He wasn't going to leave the boat behind. He would do it quietly and quickly, unnoticed if possible, and would explain only if he had to. No matter what had happened, surely Erin couldn't object. She would see what he was doing, and there would be no need for explanation; she knew how much the boat meant to him. She would be happy to see him take it away.

The jeep seemed to drive itself, knowing the way and loyally proceeding ahead with both dread and resolved determination. As he rounded the curve just before the marina, Mike saw the car pulling out of the parking lot and immediately slowed down. The black Lincoln Navigator was so common in suburbs of South Florida, it would almost serve as traffic camouflage. But down in the Keys, it stood out, and immediately caught Mike's eye.

"Gut instinct" is perhaps one of the most amorphous terms in the English language. Survivors used it when describing a premonition or perception that facilitated their survival. The wounded often used it to explain something they ignored prior to being injured. Cops used it when they suspected something but didn't have proof to substantiate their claims. Spiritual leaders described it when they talked about faith. Mike had never heard anyone deny the existence of the experience but, then again, the lost and the dead never got to throw in their two cents on the issue.

He did not turn into the marina but, instead, began following the vehicle based on what could only be described as gut instinct. He did not recognize the car, but somehow it seemed familiar. In the seconds it took him to drive past the marina parking lot, he had already come to regret his decision. It made no sense, and he chided himself as Rusty's words echoed in the back of his mind.

What if it was her new boyfriend, in his brand-new shiny pimpmobile; what was Mike going to do about it? *Probably a fucking lawyer,* he thought. But what would it help to know what he looked like, what he did, or where he lived? Erin couldn't have been any clearer and if there was any hope left, it wasn't to be found in following this car leaving her parking lot. *I should've just gotten the boat...*

I'd probably have it in the back of the jeep by now... He wondered if Erin was in the car.

There were three cars between them as they drove southward in the left lane of the four-lane divided highway. The big black behemoth was easy to spot in traffic dominated by smaller cars, mostly of a lighter color to deflect the Florida sun. He let the gap increase until there were five or six cars between them. There was only a narrow strip of land on either side of the highway, populated with high-priced waterfront property of one kind or the other, and the Navigator would have been hard to lose even for an untrained surveillant. If Erin was in the car, it was unlikely she'd ever see the jeep that far back in the mirror.

Leaving Key Largo, they drove past Tavernier and then through Plantation Key. As they moved through Islamorada, Mike wondered if they might be heading over the long bridges to the airport at Marathon; maybe the guy had his own airplane. Or maybe they were headed all the way to Key West.

With every passing mile, Mike's gut instinct slowly gave way to an appreciation of how stupid and desperate his actions were. Just as he resolved to turn the jeep around, he saw the Navigator move into the left lane and the left turn signal come on. Mike drove past the car as it turned into the Holiday Isle Resort and Marina. He memorized the car's tag number as he passed in the right lane and crossed over Whale Harbor channel before he pulled into the parking lot of a Dunkin' Donuts.

"What now, Sam Spade?" the demons in his head cackled. "You are such a pussy. You follow them for forty minutes and then, when you get the opportunity to confront them, you just drive by wide-eyed, like the lost little boy that you are."

"Just when I thought you couldn't get any more pitiful..." the big one said. "Do something ... anything ... run away if you have to, but it's embarrassing to see you keep coming back to be bitch-slapped like a eunuch. Here's an idea sissy, why don't you just drive the jeep off the bridge. No one will know the truth, and we can finally move on to someone more worthy."

Mike picked up his cellphone and hit the speed dial number four.

"Hillsborough Sheriff," the female voice answered.

"Ruthie?" Mike asked.

"Hey, Mike, what's up?"

"Can you run a tag for me? Didn't make a firm copy, but I think it's DVQ 399, might be DVO 399."

"Yep, stand by. First one is a 2010 Lexus RX registered to Richard Walker of Coral Gables, and the second is a 2014 Navigator registered to Prestige Auto Rental in Davie."

"Nope, one last try, maybe DVQ 899?" Mike asked.

"That one is a 2002 Toyota Corolla registered to Tamara DeMathis," the dispatcher responded.

"Ah, screw it, I'll go double-check. It's nothing urgent. Thanks, and have a good weekend girl."

It was a precaution he had learned from his first field

training officer after entering on duty with Hillsborough PD. If you didn't have a strong justification for why you were tracing the tag number, always build in some wiggle room in case someone asked somewhere down the road. The lack of clarity in the number would leave plenty of room for doubt and lack of memory should it turn out to be important later on. Chances were Ruthie had never entered the inquiry into the logs, but they'd still be there in the computer if anyone ever went that far.

The Lincoln Navigator he had been following was rented from a company about an hour north of Miami. "Holy shit, stop the presses!" The voices in his head laughed. "Detective Kelly has identified the vehicle as a rental. The mystery is solved, and the sleuth has won! I'm sure now that someone else won't be parting his girlfriend's legs this very evening; unless, of course, he is parting those tan legs at this very moment as Detective Kelly sits in his car, flaccid as a baby."

He had known it was stupid three seconds after he started following the car. Rusty was right, no good was to come of his hanging around. The thought of Rusty somehow strengthened him. He took a deep breath, and, without his knowledge or permission, his right hand made the sign of a cross over his body. He headed north on U.S. 1 and kept his eyes straight ahead as he passed the Holiday Isle Resort and Marina. He would get his boat and go home, leaving the past to the past.

XXV

The sandy gravel parking lot of Obduro Marina was almost empty when Mike pulled in. The young girl Erin had hired to run the store was locking the front door. He was embarrassed that he couldn't remember her name, while somehow remembering that she was Salvadoran.

Mike approached slowly as old reflexes kicked in. His eyes scanned in every direction other than the girl who was approaching him. It was happy hour on Friday, and the quiet was overwhelming. There was no music, no lights, nobody. The place was deserted.

The girl approached distraught "Mr. Mike, I'm sorry, but I didn't know what to do. I called Mr. Rusty, and he said to cancel the band and lock the store. I am very sorry." Was she crying?

"What happened, where is Erin?"

"I don't know. She is not here. She has not been here all day." The girl looked at him, big brown eyes full of water and apprehension; she buried her face into his chest and began to shudder as she tried to suppress her crying.

"Maria," the name came to Mike without thinking, "what happened?"

"Two men came. I don't know them, Ms. Erin wasn't here. I think …" She sobbed. "I think they killed the dog."

Mike held her away, holding her shoulders, looking at her eyes. "Maria, what did you see?"

She could only cry but nodded in the direction of the boat ramp, where Mike saw a pile of tan fur. He let go of her shoulders and walked over slowly, suppressing his own feelings, trying to put on the mask he assumed whenever he walked onto a crime scene.

He knelt next to Jeep the dog, flies buzzing around a mortal wound that had caved in one side of his head. Maria moaned with grief. "I found him in the water after the men left. He was floating in the water. I pulled him out, but he was dead."

"It's okay, Maria. I will take care of him; everything will be all right." He stood and gave her a hug. He held her face and looked into her eyes and, with a calm confidence owned only by the insane and doomed, reassured her, "It's going to be all right. I'll take care of Jeep. I'll take care of everything. You come back tomorrow, and it'll be fine, you'll see. But please don't talk about it with anyone else; it might hurt Ms. Erin's business."

"Gracias … gracias, Senor Mike, lo siento … mucho, gracias…" she said, still quivering, and then turned and walked away.

Hard coral rock lies six inches below the sandy surface throughout the Florida Keys, and gravesites are not dug by one man. Behind Erin's house, Mike dug as deep a hole as he could, placed Jeep the dog in the hole, and covered him with sand and then many, many rocks and stones. In an eerie silence, with only the mangrove swamps watching, he cried woefully.

XXVI

Mike sat on the gravel next to the pile of stones and stared at the little boat his older brother had built and never sailed. He thought of John and remembered how they had lowered his body into a hole, just as he had done with Jeep the dog. Good souls now forever gone. And the graves were getting shallower.

He had no plan as he got into the car and headed south. Something inside had changed. He no longer felt the sense of loss or grief. In fact, he felt nothing. And he thought of nothing. The game clock had stopped and, if he had thought of it, he would have had no idea how long it had taken him to drive back down to the parking lot of the Holiday Isle Marina. He cruised through the parking lot and continued past the Lincoln Navigator without a second glance, parking the jeep at the far end of the lot. He sat for a minute, not thinking, not reflecting, not waiting, not planning … maybe wishing he was someplace else. He opened the glove box and pulled out his service weapon, a Glock model 17 held in a holster specifically designed to be tucked inside the belt for concealment. He checked the magazine for a full load of over a dozen 9-mm rounds. He got out of the jeep and tucked the gun inside the back right side of his belt.

He walked around the north side of the resort and entered the famous Tiki Bar area in the back of the property. The weekend debauchery was just beginning, and both the locals and the tourists seemed in a hurry to get a load on. It was one of the largest resorts in the Central Keys, and a wet T-shirt contest was about to start at one of the three outside bars. He took a weary seat at the far corner of the most remote bar and ordered a Budweiser as he scanned the crowd, not knowing what he was looking for.

He sat nursing his beer for forty-five minutes, watching the alcohol sweep away the worries and inhibitions of the revelers, providing a temporary relief that he knew all too well. Drinking had lost its joy for Mike since John's death; it was a dark and cold place to which he fled in weakness. But these were happy drinkers, engaged in loud and expressive social intercourse, looking to make new friends and memories. Watching them was tiresome, and the growing crowd made him nervous. While he didn't know what he was looking for, he knew it wasn't here. He decided to look around some of the several guest buildings.

Without a plan, his instincts drove him to the outer edges, the shadows of the stairwell rather than the confines of the elevator, avoiding eye contact while still slowly flowing as if he had somewhere to go. After surveying three of the seven buildings, he decided to check the parking lot and see if the Navigator was even still there.

He saw them as soon as he walked out of the building facing the front parking lot. Closing the tailgate of the Navigator, the two men were each carrying a small suitcase. He stopped short, before leaving the shadow of the building, and let the images soak in. As was his custom, he gave them nicknames and guessed that "Skipper" was a little over six feet, big belly, probably 240 pounds. Full head of black curly hair, dress slacks and tucked-in shirt, he was no local. "Gilligan" was probably five foot ten, 170 pounds, lighter skin, with a ball cap and a goatee. Both were wearing leather shoes. Skipper had a slight limp and, while not staggering, their gate implied they had been imbibing.

Mike followed from the shadows. The two were talking and occasionally laughing, completely relaxed and oblivious to their environs. Skipper switched his bag from one hand to the other as they walked down the front sidewalk, past one building and then another, absorbed in their banter. As they approached building seven, the southernmost, it suddenly dawned on Mike that they might be leading him into a trap, and he quickly made a scan to see if anyone was following him as he stalked Skipper and Gilligan. The music echoed from the party on the backside of the buildings, but there was no one else in front of the building.

They walked through the first-floor open-air foyer of the building and, as they passed the stairs, Mike began to pick up his pace, entering the foyer just in time to see them turn to the left. He made a left turn, exiting the foyer, and saw that the two were already entering the second room to the left of the foyer. There were lights facing out toward the party area, but Mike had gone blind to everything but his prey.

He entered the hotel room just as Gilligan was letting the door swing shut. Sweeping in, one foot up on the bed, he came down and forward onto Gilligan's shoulders with every ounce of strength he had, driving the man onto his knees and into the back of Skipper's legs. Skipper turned around to see what the hell was going on and quickly focused on the gun that was pointing at his head.

"On your knees, looking away from me," Mike said. Skipper complied.

"Yo, take it easy, jefe, no need to fight … money and credit cards all in the billfold, right rear pocket, just relax with the gatt, man," Skipper said with a Spanish accent. Gilligan was coming out of his daze and, on his hands and knees, turned to see what had hit him.

"I don't want your fucking money. You two kill the dog?"

"Dog?? What fucking dog? What the fuck you hit me like that for?" Gilligan said. A street punk who wanted to be Black or Hispanic, or anything cooler than what he was.

"No, jefe, we ditint kill Dog; we ditint kill nobody. We

don't even know which "Dog" you talkin' about, but we ditint kill nobody." The Spanish accent sounded like it was Jersey Cuban.

"Tell me why you killed the dog."

"Fuck you, asshole, we didn't kill no one," Gilligan said, starting to rise up. "You got the wrong guys, and you better—"

Taking his finger off the trigger, Mike brought the butt of the gun down hard against the back of Gilligan's head. One step forward, past the slumped body of Gilligan, Mike delivered a forceful kick right between Skipper's legs, sending the big man all the way down to the carpet on his side, grabbing his crotch.

XXVII

Mike casually pulled out their billfolds, returned to the hotel room door, threw the deadbolt and slid the chain into its hasp. He sat down in the chair with his back to the window and stared down in surprise at the shining silver badges of Detectives Florencio and Thompson of the Fort Lauderdale Police Department. He pulled out an American Express platinum card from each wallet, comparing them and confirming they were identical. He glanced over an alias driver's license contained in each wallet, high quality, like those issued for undercover work.

He immediately got back up and frisked Gilligan, who was starting to moan, and took the small Glock 26 subcompact out of his ankle holster. He moved up to Skipper and pulled a larger gun out of the holster inside the back of his pants. Bigger man, bigger gun ... and too big to be doing all that bending over and drawing from the ankle shit. Mike put the guns in his own pants pockets and sat back down, further inspecting the credentials. He stared silently at the two, knowing he was missing something—that he knew something he had not yet put together.

Gilligan regained consciousness and was holding the large lump on the back of his head. The moaning from his partner had diminished, but he was still holding his crotch with both hands.

"You okay, Flo?" Gilligan asked.

"I'll make it … he kicked me in the fucking balls … motherfucker," he said, looking at Mike.

Mike just stared at them, letting the silence have its effect. "So, Detectives, care to tell me what brings you to the lovely Holiday Isle? Honeymoon, maybe?"

"You loco, papi? Now you know we're cops, you know how much trouble you're in. What you hanging around for? You gonna take our stuff, go ahead, we'll come find you. You want to shoot us, go ahead, but maybe shoot yourself too, cause there only one road in and one road out—nowhere to hide down here you shoot two cops."

"Like I said …" Mike continued, ignoring the challenge, "what brings you to this part of the woods?" now slowing down his speech, adding some fake southern drawl.

"Enough with the stupid questions, pato, you gonna do something, do it!" Agitated, trying to shake something loose, trying to assess his opponent, but still not rising off the floor or making any moves.

"Wait up, Flo," Gilligan says. "I remember this guy … you're the guy—you're the guy looking for an open bar this morning."

"That's right, Detective. Which brings us back once more to my initial question: what are you doing down here, and why the fuck were you following me this morning?"

"Ah, shit, dog, that's what this is all about?" says Gilligan. "You didn't have to rough us up like that, bro; you coulda just asked. This is classified, but, since you holding a gun an' everything, guess I can tell you. We're working a narcotics investigation. Saw you leaving the business of our suspect, and thought we'd see what you were up to, man. You just getting an early buzz on baby ... no harm, no foul. Why don't you just give us back our shit, and we'll just forget about everything, cool?"

"Why don't you tell me about your investigation?"

"Really, bro? Like I said, we thought you might be involved, but we past that. You don't wanna know 'bout our investigation; it'll just cause problems for you." Gilligan talking all sweet and syrupy, Skipper starting to feel a little better, sitting up but not saying anything, letting his partner do the talking.

Mike held the gun up in front of his face, appearing to inspect it, then looking back at Gilligan.

"Okay, man, you wanna know, you can know. There's a bitch owns the marina we seen you leavin' this morning. She been picking up bales dropped off in the water at night by planes coming in from the Islands. We just about got the case wrapped up too—planning on arresting her today or tomorrow. You happy? Now you know our case, you can go call the *Inquirer*. Or maybe we gonna think again 'bout chargin' you with something."

Mike looks up at the ceiling, like he's trying to figure things out, taking his time, just like Colombo used to do.

"She's bringing in dope... down here in the Keys ... how's that involve Fort Lauderdale PD?"

Gilligan pauses. Just a second, but they both know it. Now acting upset "Fuck bro, this is complicated shit; it's a three volume case, you want the whole story, let's go up north, and I'll get you the case files. That be okay? What the fuck is it to you anyway?"

"And I gotta wonder why you're driving a rented Lincoln Navigator, not your service vehicle ... this being work and all..."

XXVIII

The light of recognition goes off in their eyes at the same time. "You're a cop?" says Skipper, the first coherent words spoken since he was kicked in the nuts.

"This is how it generally works in these situations, Detectives: the guy with the gun gets to ask the questions, and guys without the guns have to answer them."

"Give us back our shit right now mother-fucker, or your job and pension are gone, and you gonna land up butt-raped twice a day in Raiford." More than anger... outrage, humiliation, disgust, all at once. But still not enough to forget who's holding the guns.

Gilligan takes a different approach. "That bitch ... she got you to comin' after us, bro? That what she think she gonna do? You think you gonna scare us off? Fuck you and fuck her; we ain't leaving till we get what we came for."

"And what exactly is that, Detective Thompson? What did you come for?"

The silence hangs for a few seconds before Skipper tries to cover up. "Yeah, papi, you a thinkin' man, maybe she serve up some shit and tell you it's flan, right? We know her. She used to be a confidential informant for us, but she likes the drugs too much, and she lies too much, and now we found out 'bout this pick-up business she runnin', we gotta bring her in ourselves. You a cop, jefe, you know how it is with snitches. Gotta finish the job is all."

"Of course I understand; you wouldn't mind if I called your office and confirmed your investigation with your supervisor—what's his name?"

More silence. Making up a cover story on the fly is difficult, especially if you're used to being the one holding the badge and asking the questions. Too hard for Gilligan.

"Fuck this—what she paying you, dawg? We can double it. She probably ain't gonna pay you anyway."

"How much does she owe you?"

"Mo' than she can afford, dawg. On the real, whatever she paying you, we double it."

"How'd she get it outta you?"

"Damn, dog, you ask a lotta questions. What she tell you? Even though I know it wasn't the truth."

"So I take it you don't want me to call your supervisors?"

"She took something of ours …" Skipper pipes up, trying to cover again for his quick-lipped partner. "… well, not really ours … something we were watching for somebody. Like a security detail, you know, papi? Make us look real bad. We jus' gotta get it back is all, nothing wrong with that, right? We gonna get a little finder's fee, you know, like Randy say, we can cut you in on that action."

"What'd she take?"

"You and these fuckin' questions, bro! She hired you, what'd she tell you we looking for?"

"A boat."

"Yeah, bitch told the truth about that! A very big boat. Bitch stoled a boat from the po'lice; we can't tolerate that, you know how it is."

"She said you tried to rape her."

"You can't rape a bitch that's givin' it away, man! She a dope-sucking snitch that fucked with the wrong guys. We gonna get back what she stole; you want in on the action or not?"

"She ain't got the boat."

"Yeah, we know that too. But she got that marina, and it's doing some fine business now. Be worth more than that fucking boat to our friend, he needs a business like that. She's all set to sign it over Monday morning. You don't need do nothing, man, just take your cut an' walk away. She learn her lesson 'bout fucking with the po'lice and everybody walk away happy-happy, bro."

"Your friend, he the guy gave you the platinum credit cards?"

The two of them looking at each other, no idea what to say. "Yeah, papi, you figured it out, you a smart cop. He a bad man though … you thinkin' 'bout cutting us out? He won't talk to you, jefe."

"He know about the girl?"

No hesitation this time. "Jefe, like I say, he a bad man. He knew about the girl, he'd come and get what's his on his own, *no need for me and Randy. Just us three now, papi, like the Three Musketeers."*

"Car and hotel on his credit card?"

"Yeah, jefe, but why you thinkin' on it so hard? It's easy papi; you don't need to do nothing but let it happen. We give you a full third, we ain't even gotta know your name or nothin'. All done Monday morning and go our different ways. Like Randy say, it's a lot more than whatever she say she gonna pay you … and we ain't gonna back off anyways. Not like you no boyscout yourself papi, takin' money from her. Our money just bigger."

Tipping back in chair, feigning a smile "I think we can find a solution here, gentlemen. But I don't trust you, and I'm not comfortable with the way you do things. You're not going to like this, but we're going back to the girl's place. Where are your handcuffs?"

I call the front desk and check out of the room, tell the clerk to go ahead and charge the credit card. The two lie facedown on the ground and I handcuff their inside arms together. They pick up their bags with their outside hands as we walk outside, "Look like you're in love, boys, anyone gets suspicious and the tent falls in on all of us."

They walk toward the Navigator. "Nope, we're gonna be taking my ride," directing them to the jeep. "but that reminds me, which one of you has the keys to the Lincoln?" I reach inside Skipper's front right pocket and pull out the keys.

XXIX

The ride to the marina is quick and uneventful. Gilligan bitches about having to lean over while Skipper drives, Me sitting behind them saying nothing.

The marina is deserted, and I point toward the docks.

"Whoa, papi, this not wat you said, we gonna talk to the girl, remember?" I say nothing, but push the big man in the direction of the old skiff Rusty and I had taken out so long ago.

Their steps are slow, bargaining for every inch between them and the boat. Gilligan starts jabbering and looking around real quick, like an addict looking for a fix. But we all know who has the guns, and we all step slowly into the boat.

"Up in the bow."

"Papi, theenk about wat you doing, man. Why? Our boy ain't gonna deal with you, he don't know you—you need us. Mira, you want all the money, is okay, but we still got to introduce you to our boy, won't work any other way. You can have all the money, I swear, but this is no good papi, please."

Fucking Gilligan never shuts up either, jabbering, desperate, both of them. Men are dangerous when they think they are about to die. I have the gun in the open now, not taking my eyes off the two, I feel under the console, find the key and fire up the boat.

Gun up and sights in on Gilligan. "Untie the bowline."

"Fuck you, bro! Just go ahead and shoot me then, if that's what you up to; you think I give a shit? You'll be hunted down for the piece of crap you are. I got——"

The sound of the shot echoes briefly off the water but is quickly eaten up by the mangroves. I nod toward the bowline again, and the two get up as Gilligan unties it. I do the same at the stern and turn the spotlight so that it shines in the eyes of the two cops, but also lights up where I'm headed.

The chart plotter is working, but getting out of the swamp channel is all visual. The two cops are looking at each other and whispering. I pull hard back on the throttle and the boat surges and settles; the two knocked on their asses. All parties looking at each other but nothing said.

Throttle back up and almost clear the channel, kill the spotlight and the running lights. Moon is out and its fifteen feet between them and me. Throttle now full speed as I glance back and forth between the chart plotter and the bad men, my gun now back in my pocket. They will try me and they have weight on their side. Coordination is their weakness, being chained together. At this speed all I have to do is tilt the wheel and they're both out of the boat. Talking again and they're getting set, jerk the wheel hard left and right and they know they can't traverse the distance if I see them coming.

Time has lost its measure as we approach the Thousand Islands. Spotlight back on as I look at the chart plotter for the deepest channel in. Slower now, and more stable, they can charge but they are blinded by the spotlight and don't know exactly where I am. Slower, shallower, twisting, turning, slower, shallower, and then the bump into the sand.

"Here's the keys boys, unlock yourselves and get out," spotlight still on them.

"We ain't getting out here, motherfucker, this is the fuckin' everglades. Fuck you! You wanna kill us bro, just do it and get it over, but we ain't getting eaten up alive by some fuckin' alligator."

He continues to babble on but eventually they unlock the handcuffs and get out on the starboard bow, spotlight following them. They got light so they can see where they're going, water knee-deep. Looking for dry land, a safe port in a storm, something to hang on to.

Skipper turns slowly after the gunshot and looks down at Gilligan, half covered by water, his life blood turning the marsh water around him darker in the artificial light. Looking up at me he waits a moment and I put him down. I walk forward and pick up the handcuffs and keys. I throw them and the guns into the water near the bodies and a predator splashes. The feeding has already begun.

XXX

She is there when I come in, standing outside her house, a silhouette in lamplight. Her hands reach up and cover her face, she is crying. I tie up the boat and put the key exactly back where I had found it. I look around, slowly now, there is no rush, and there is nothing left of the trip or the occupants.

I walk up the dock and along the side of the store. She is barefoot and wearing a long nightshirt, her hands still covering her beautiful face, crying inconsolably. I look at the shed containing my brother's boat and my own eyes become clouded and my throat hard. I look back at Erin and I want to say you won't have to worry about those particular bad men anymore … but I know I am one of them and say nothing. I get in my jeep and drive north.

"Hey."

"Hey, it's Mike." Silence.

"Was wondering if you still had friends in the car disposal business?" Silence.

"Yeah." More silence. "But I go to jail if I get caught. And

at my age, that's where I'll die." More silence.

"It's a Navigator in the Holiday Isle parking lot. Black. Keys are in Erin's boat. Need the car to be out of state in two days. Complete chop, no re-sale."

"I'll handle it. You have my word, the car won't exist in forty-eight hours. What scrap is left won't be closer than Alabama."

"Rusty, I wouldn't ask if I thought it would go south on you."

"I know … it's just that I told you to leave, that no good would come of hanging around here."

"Yeah … I know…" my tired throat fights back tears that my eyes won't produce "… they shouldn't have killed the dog."

"Rusty?" No answer. "I guess I'm going to hell?"

"Boy, you're already there. Hang in there. I love you."

About the Author

Jim Markson retired from the CIA in 2014 after 29 years of service as an Investigator, Polygraph Examiner, and Case Officer. This is his first published book. The name Markson was originally assigned by the CIA as an alias during litigation over a prior manuscript, and the author continues to use it as a pen-name for reasons of personal privacy and security. For more information, please visit his website at www.jimmarksonauthor.com